Flowering

FLOWERING

BY

LORRAINE SHARPE

COPYRIGHT CASSELBERRY, FLORIDA 2018
BY LORRAINE VALENTIN SHARPE
All rights reserved

Edited by GEORGE FREDERICK MEYER JR.

Published by Black Oyster Publishing Co. Inc.
Grateful acknowledgement to Harper & Row, publishers
and Mary Helen Washington, copyright 1990 for"They're Eyes
Were Watching God by Zora Neale Hurston for frontispiece quote.
This book is entirely a work of fiction.
Names, places and incidents
found here are either a product of the
author's imagination or are used fictitiously
Similarity to actual persons is entirely coincidental.

Also by this author:

GRACE MAP
by Lorraine Valentin Sharpe, 2002

DIRTY FEET
by Lorraine Valentin Sharpe Meyer, 2010

AT SEA
by Lorraine Sharpe 2016

Flowering

Lorraine Sharpe

I DEDICATE THIS BOOK

TO THE POTPOURRI OF WISE AND BEAUTIFUL WOMEN

ALL OF MY
SISTERS-IN-LAW, DAUGHTERS-IN-LAW,
NEICES, COUSIN, GRANDDAUGHTERS, STEPDAUGHTERS
AND FRIENDS

AND ESPECIALLY IN MEMORY OF JOYCE

HOW FORTUNATE I AM

Flowering

She pulled in her horizon like a great fish net.
Pulled it from around the waist of the world
and draped it over her shoulder
So much of life was in its meshes.

                        Zora Neale Hurston

Flowering

FLOWERING

CHAPTER 1

I realized too suddenly as I held his drooping lifeless head, that I was starving.

Jaum's parents weren't even surprised when another child of their's died. Both of them, shoulders hanging, the lines in their tan faces worn downward, expressionless, not a tear or sound from either of them. Jaum's mother, Weelai fell to the clinic's cement floor, landing in a squat position, her normally strong legs too weak to hold up the weight of her sadness. Jaum's father fondled the boy's callused feet as he must have done ten years ago when he held his newborn boy, checking to see that all the toes were there. All the while I, the nurse who was supposed to be their support, the professional, could not control my sobbing. I lay down the sweat-wet head of this emaciated boy. I had seen him laughing as he rode a buffalo to the clinic only a few days before but somehow I had missed noticing that his olive skin looked more white and his eyes more yellow than they were meant to be. Hookworm should not have stolen this child's wonderful life. He could have been a scientist or a doctor or even a dad, someday.

As I tried to compose myself, that dear grieving father lay his son's feet down on the bed, stepped over to me, put his hands together before his face as if in prayer, bowed to me and said in the few English words he could muster, "Suung, you go home now. Too sad. You go see Papa. You need Papa."

He was right, it was time for me to leave this village. I did not come here eight years ago to stay. I thought it would be an adventure. Maybe I'd meet the woman of my dreams in Thailand, working for the Peace Corps. Maybe I'd fall in love with a person who had the same ideals as myself so that we together, could spend our lives doing good for people in need. Maybe none of this would happen but I'd return home to Oklahoma in a few months, a more interesting person than I had been before my travel and experience.

Now, at thirty-six years of age, was there even time for me to start my life over again? These bamboo, cane and dried leaf homes, sometimes bereft of any furnishings, smiling people sometimes toothless, playing children, sometimes naked, gentle friends, always wise, were the closest thing I had to a family. I had put off any serious thought of leaving here but I knew I could not escape a gut-wrenching decision much longer. Did I want to make my forever home here in Muang Iai? I had not painted a landscape or portrait in all these years and I was an artist. I had lost my sense of beauty and filled the emptiness of my emotions and psyche with pain and sadness. Oh, the native people knew how to deal with their poverty and hunger, but I did not. I tried so hard to be one of them, to accommodate, to "thailandize" myself, but never filled the space in my spirit with intimacy or laughter.

The Thai villagers could not remember my name, Aubrey, so they named me Suung meaning tall. My height, five feet, ten inches, was the characteristic of mine that most stood out for them. I was not just a Farang, or foreigner. I was not Sidam, even though I had milk chocolate skin or Khunlaw for my outstanding handsomeness. I was not Iai for the big footprint I made or Graeng, for my strong basketball-champion-like shoulders and slim neck nor even Pyaban because I was a nurse or Chai Pyaban for being a male nurse. The villagers said what they saw with no inhibition and never as a criticism. They welcomed the novelty that was me with warm curiosity.

After Jaum's death and his father's wise counsel, I delayed a decision again, distracting myself as I had so many times before. The village was ready to explode into the festival of Loi Krathong. Each year I joined the villagers' trudge through swampy weeds in search of the largest, most scented flower. Bringing our prize back to the clinic we worked all day to bolster up the center of the flower with other greens in a basket weave so that it was possible to stand a candle in its center. After dark we all headed to the rivers edge with our flowers-holding-lit-candles and placed them on the flowing water.

Flowering

According to ancient Buddhist tradition the flowers and their scent represent beauty, the lit candle, enlightenment or wisdom, the merging of the candled flowers on the water represent oneness of the people and universe and the disappearance of the candles as they move downstream represent, our passage together to eternity. When the light from the candles had faded, and the flowering of our lives had been symbolized, we all moved to the center of town to make merry in a never ending festival. The festival of Loi Krathong night is held in the town center. There was no town center as a United States American would know a town. The place "we" in Muang Iai called town was like the baseball field of an American park surrounded by homemade temporary stands set up for a festival occasion. There the townspeople bartered and sold every kind of food that they had created for each other. There were rice deserts and rice appetizers and rice entrees. There were little barbecued sparrows, head feet and all. You held the sparrow by the feet and bit off its head. There was snake meat and there were many fruits: papaya, mango, lychee, durian and rambutan. Some of the fruit like the large durian smelled bad to western sense but tasted delicious; some smelled great, but the taste, whew! The juice of all of the fruits ran down your chin and dripped onto your clothes, a sign that you were relishing the fruit and their culture. No paper napkins. If one said they liked Thai food they were labeled "very clever" by the villagers.

The field was lighted by candles that were posted at each food stand. The festival's loud and scratchy Asian music competed with laughter and dancing, plenty of sound. The air was saturated with the scent of burning ginger and coconut curry and the bodies of a few hundred people who had no means of bathing. The sensation overload and hilarity would last long into the night.

Loi Krathong lasts for a week, during which the Thai people throw water at each other, symbolizing their continued oneness and gratitude for each other and for the gift of water. In the market, on the train if your window is open, as you head to school or work, you could expect to be soaked by strangers. You bowed and greeted the stranger and laughed along with them. Always in Thailand, you had to be a good sport, even if a wet good sport..

After a week of this, the festival was over. The next distraction for me would be Christian Christmas which was staid and boring in comparison to Thai festivals. How long would I distract myself with events instead of facing my fear of loneliness? I had no immediate family to return to. I had persuaded myself that I needed a few days to get past the sadness of losing Jaum before I could think objectively about leaving here. I had taken months. Is such a decision ever objective? Not in a million years, but nevertheless, it was time for a decision. It was not lychee nuts and rice for which I was starving.

And so I did it, I left this clinic that I had helped build, the people and country that had been my whole life.

I packed my few souvenirs, the personal gifts that these dear people had given to me from their dearth, reminders of the last eight years of my life. The villagers gathered in front of the clinic the morning I departed. They presented me with a community's gift, one that they had worked on for many months in anticipation of my departure. They had known better than I did that I would be leaving soon.

Their gift was a yellow and pink Thai silk pasin or sarong. In their village they had raised the worms, collected the cocoons, pulled and wound the silk thread, dyed it in the klong or canal and woven it into heavy silk. This would be my most precious possession. Everything else I owned I had fit into one bag, shorts, jeans, lightweight shirts, a few sweaters, sandals and a windbreaker, all that I had brought with me eight years ago when I came to work with the people in the village of Muang Iai planning to stay for a few months.

When Brother Philip picked me up to drive me to the airport I turned quickly and jumped into his truck so that the villagers wouldn't see the tears running down my cheeks. Would I ever see them again? They, I think knew the irony of their farewell when they called out, "Hurry back Suung."

From the airport I called Cecily, the only still single friend I had in the States with whom I had kept in touch. "Aubrey! Where are you? Is anything wrong?" She asked.

I answered, "Cecily, I'm leaving Thailand. Yes, actually leaving, as in moving back to the States. May I come there first to visit you in Oregon?"

"Of course you can visit me," she replied. "Can you stay awhile? Stay here with me. Stay as long as you like, I have plenty of room for you."

"Good thing you said 'yes' because I already have a ticket for Portland," I said. "In fact I'm waiting now to board the plane." I hurried the conversation. I didn't want to get into a whole discussion about my reasons for returning to the States.

"Aubrey, when do you land? Can I meet your plane?" Cecily asked.

I discouraged her from meeting me in Portland. " Cecily, even though they call this a direct flight, it stops in Hawaii for the passengers to go through customs there. We all have to get off, go through the customs gates, then get back on and return to our previous seats. We can't even leave the airport during the stop over. Customs should take about two hours. Then we continue on to Portland. Since I don't change planes, it should be smooth sailing, or flying that is, from Hawaii to Portland. Maybe the reason for the stop in Hawaii is refueling or something. We should get to Portland about seven in the morning. The timing is too uncertain though. What if something detains us in Hawaii? I don't want you to be sitting in the airport waiting.

"Anyway, I think it would be fun for me to take the train from Portland to Seaside like I used to do," I told her. "I'll call you from Portland when I have a train reservation. Then you can pick me up at the Seaside Train Depot. Okay?"

"Okay. Aubrey I can't wait to hear your story, but you better catch that plane now. We'll have all the time we want to talk about stuff when you get here. I'll be waiting for your call tomorrow."

CHAPTER 2

The emotional upheaval I had experienced in the last three months since I had decided to leave Thailand took its toll on me as I began my trip homeland, that is, back to the United States of America. I had been born there, in Broken Bow, Oklahoma. My father raised sheep. Born in slums of Nigeria, he was happy with his country life, his wife, his farm and his sheep and wide open spaces. The only thing I know he missed, was having a house full of children. I was his one and only, but he would say I was enough.

My mother had been a small town girl. She learned to cook, to knit, to do needle work to bake and to clean house at her mother's knee. I think that having only one child had not been as hard on her as on my dad. Her life seemed fully satisfied with her acre sized vegetable garden that fed half of the town, her chickens, her household chores and community events. But when farming became too hard on my Dad, they both agreed that it was time for them to see the world. They happily sold their sheep farm, bought a small motor home and hit the road.

By that time, I was gone from home. It wasn't just that I wanted to escape rural living. In fact, I've continued to be most comfortable in towns that hold just enough people for me to call them all by name. But I wanted to be a nurse. I always wanted to be a nurse from the time when, at the age of seven I met my first nurse. That's when I broke my foot jumping from the barn rafter and ended up in a hospital. The nurse who took care of me and told me how brave and strong I was, looked to me like Mohammed Ali.

After completing my nursing education in Tulsa, I applied for and was accepted in the Master's degree program in Geriatrics at UCLA. I completed this degree in the minimal time one and a half years. Living in Los Angeles didn't appeal to me though, too much traffic, too few friends out of so many people. So I was on the move again.

Next I moved to Portland, Oregon. The only reason I chose Portland was a job offer I found there that sounded interesting. It was a position in home care nursing, specializing in rehabilitation of people with stroke, Parkinson's Disease, joint replacements and support for families of people suffering from dementia. It also offered as one of its benefits, endless paid further education. That sounded like an adventure to me even though I already had all the degrees I wanted. My parents were chomping at the bit to travel. Having my own adventure it seemed to me, would free them from any concern they might have about "being there for me." I loved them dearly and wanted to give them their freedom. They could always visit me in Oregon on one of their road trips.

While living in Portland and at the expense of my employer, I took numerous night school courses just for fun. At the time, I had no ambition to climb the ladder, look for better jobs. This job was the best. Anything I could learn about the big wide world by going to school, would make me better at my job. I would be a more interesting person for my patients. It was hard enough for them to have professional people intruding on their world. At least when they had to put up with me, I could stimulate their imaginations.

On one of my summer ventures, I signed up for a course in Anthropology at the school of Public Health at Lewis and Clark College. As I sat in the rear of the classroom gazing around at the other students, I saw a blond head bobbing around in front of me with a kind of tilt that brought back a memory. Could it be? Another person from Broken Bow? In Portland? No, it couldn't. But when class was over and we were all gathering our notes and books, I walked over closer to see her.

"Cecily?"

"Aubrey?"

Then we said together: "What are you doing here? I can't believe it."

And so we each found a childhood friend in a totally unexpected place. Cecily had a blond pony tail, slight bits of makeup, mostly accenting her blue eyes, simple pearl earrings. She was wearing jeans, a red tee and navy sandals, the 'uniform' of our peers. She looked tired.

I knew nothing of her circumstances, only that she had moved away from Broken Bow sometime during our high school years. I had never really forgotten about her because we had shared a sheep at one time, in the 4H club that we both had belonged to. Cecily had been like a sister to me then, since neither of us had siblings. Raising a sheep, learning to feed it, care for it, shear it was so much more fun with a buddy than it would have been alone. A partner was someone who would laugh at your goofy looking bad shearing job.

I too had worn jeans and tee to class, changing clothes quickly in the bathroom of the school after coming from work.

"Cecily let's go someplace together so we can talk. It's been so long. I just can't believe its you," I said.

"Aubrey, I'd love to, but I really can't tonight. How about before our class on Thursday? We could meet at the Brewery right down the street from here at the corner. 5:00 P.M."

"You're on. My treat," I said. "I can't wait."

We walked out together, she turning left out of the door, I turned right to walk back to my apartment, never asking about where each other lived. There would be time for that.

It wasn't until after our third meeting that I discovered that Cecily was in dire straits. She was staying in a raunchy motel on the nights of our classes. She couldn't afford better and it saved her from driving the two hours home in the dark. She was working her way through college, determined to have a career of independence and proprietorship.

Eventually Cecily moved in with me so that she could be safer and could save the motel money. During those short years I learned more about her story, about the child she gave birth to during her high school years and about her being forced to move away from the Oklahoma farm. After finishing her schooling she moved up to Seaside, Oregon started earning money as a bartender while she searched for her dream job.

I dated several women casually. Then I met Casey, a therapist at my home care agency. We were seeing each other regularly and enjoyably, when I found an ad in The American Journal of Nursing for a temporary nursing position at Muang Iai, in northern Thailand. Casey was as excited as I was for me to have this adventure. It would offer me experience in tropical diseases and in village living. The Thai language would present a barrier but surely I would be provided with an interpreter. The time there would be too short for even a crash course in this difficult language.

I would ask for a brief extension of the one month vacation that I had coming to me. The trouble is, I fell in love with Thailand. After requesting two more extensions of vacation time, I finally and willingly gave up my position in Portland. I was not so willing to give up Casey but I understood her desire to be free of me since I could not assure her that I would return soon.

Flowering

CHAPTER 3

I **had taken the first flight** available from Bangkok to Portland. The first wing of the journey, up to Hawaii was quiet enough, but I wasn't sleepy yet so I watched the clouds and blue sky and thoroughly and slowly enjoyed an airline version of American food. I had decided to sleep on the second wing of the journey but I had a new mate on the plane after stopping for customs in Hawaii. This mate was a "Gabby Hayes" who was coming from an exciting vacation in Hawaii and was determined to share every minute of it with me. First I heard about her lei on arrival at Molokai, the former home for people with leprosy. Then I heard about the pig on a spit with all the details, dripping pineapple and coconut milk. Then I heard about hula dancers and the need for sunscreen and whale watching. Lastly she even took me mentally to the ferocious assault of Pearl Harbor.

Now I was, sitting in a Portland train station waiting to board the Starlight Express headed to Seaside, Oregon, hopefully in the quiet of my lonely self. The station was cold and damp. Smelled musty. The light was too dim to read much. The people standing or sitting or restlessly standing and sitting in the station were mostly bored. All the more, the little girl and boy waiting to board probably going to visit grandparents, stood out in their dress-up clothes. The little girl wore a pink dress beneath her white faux fur coat, the boy's tailored coat topped long wool pants. Their excitement was fun to watch and illustrated my mood more than the couch potato adults that surrounded me. I had an hour that turned into two hours to wait for the train after I called Cecily.

Kind of as a joke Cecily said, "I'll have a red carnation in my hair so you can recognize me, when I come to the station."

"Cecily, thank you, I said. Are you still a tall beautiful blond? I don't think I'll have any trouble recognizing you and you'll know me, I'm sure. I'll probably be the only black dude in Seaside. If you can't find me, just look for the biggest smile." To be honest, I was a little concerned about being able to recognize Cecily after so many years.

I sat there in the Portland train station shivering in this grey, rainy January weather, I was wearing only the khaki shorts, white cotton shirt and sandals and the windbreaker, that I had worn leaving Thailand. It was a lot hotter when I left there. It is always hot in Thailand. These duds were the only kind I had to wear, besides torn jeans. I would need a lot of time to shop for clothes and right now was not that time. Right now was Seaside or bust.

I had purchased a "free" train ticket, meaning that I didn't have an assigned seat. As soon as that train whistle blew, I was going to head for the last coach car and dash through the train until I would see an empty corner window seat. I wanted to be alone. I needed to think, to plan, maybe to cry a little, maybe cry myself to sleep. Changing time zones was fatiguing. I didn't need a gabby mate like I had had on the plane.

What would my life be like now? The only reality I could touch or imagine right now was a laid back "my pen ry," as the Thai said,"never mind, tomorrow will come." My mind harked back to the big white-toothed smile of a little girl with short straight black bangs, dirty knees and bare feet sitting on a buffalo. And the man with infected, ulcerated feet, smiling while he rode his tuk tuk bicycle to earn twenty cents a day. These were the things that had been important in my life until now. I remembered how, before my arrival, the clinic building where I worked had been a church, but the villagers preferred to gather out under the space that looked like an American carport when they prayed together. Their outdoor "church" had a cement floor, aluminum uprights, roof made from rice and mud. There they could walk around the space three times to chase evil spirits away before beginning their catholic mass.

After attending several of their gatherings I had said, "Nobody knows what to do with this church building. Why don't we make it into a clinic?" The brothers and midwives and I had divided the church building into rooms, one for our make shift laboratory, one with four cots for patients to be examined or treated, one as a storehouse for drugs and supplies, throw-a-ways received from American companies that needed the tax break. We considered it a win-win. Expired medicines? Better than none.

What a different world I was entering now. I needed time to try to imagine and give credence to peer nurses sitting around a conference table. They and their concerns would have to be important now. They'd be stewing over a budget or a schedule as if the world would collapse should they make the wrong decision. The thought of the histrionics made me nauseated. Something in my new life would have to be more worthwhile than a boardroom to keep me here in the United States.

Happily, I landed the seat I wanted in the very last car of the train. Then, darn it, after the train jerked forward Tillie, a woman from three rows forward, turned around, looked at me and my empty seat, grabbed her duffle bag from the overhead bin, put on her shades and baseball cap and headed back to me, paradise lost. She dumped all five and a half feet of herself on it. "I don't want you to be alone for this whole trip," she said to me. "I can use a little company too."

I couldn't do this, couldn't sit and listen to "Miss Camouflage". I didn't want to sit and listen to other people's important problems right now. Trouble is, I've always had difficulty saying 'no' to others. So maybe I'd just have to listen for a while. I could get this over with soon if I let her talk.

Tillie was wearing camouflage shorts and a black long sleeved sweatshirt. Her auburn curly hair pulled back behind her ears made her look young for a woman of, I guessed, about thirty-five years of age. She wore hiker's boots, black socks and no makeup, no rings, no other jewelry. Her voice was deep, her eyes were shifty and her teeth were straight and white except for a chip on the right front upper. She smelled of Old Spice. To be honest, something about Tillie made me think of a walrus.

She started out telling me that she was coming from Yosemite but not where she was heading. "My train rides up and down this coast are my pastime," she said. "I get to meet all kinds of guys this way," she grinned and winked, seeming pleased with herself, like she was picturing all the handsome dudes she had enticed before this, like I was the lucky one. She had done enough self-introduction to make it seem natural for her to start asking me about myself. "Do you live in Seaside?" she asked.

Though reluctantly, I felt the need to respond to her. "No Tillie, I'm from Oklahoma but I've been living in Thailand for eight years, so I don't know anything about this area." I thought my ignorance of local gossip might discourage her from the need to converse further but it just stimulated her more.

"Well, what do you know!" she exclaimed. "You can tell me all about Thailand. That must have been very exciting."

"It was at first," I admitted. "But then I got to work, settled in you know, and it became my life. I didn't feel like a tourist. I didn't even take many pictures. I think the people did like me though. I was some kind of novelty for them. They seemed to think American medical personnel worked a kind of miracle whenever our treatments helped them feel better, because they didn't understand about antibiotics and other modern medicine. I think though, that they eventually thought of me as one of them. They even gave me a Thai nickname. They called me Suung because it means tall, and they thought of me as very tall, though I'm only five, ten."

"You're a doctor?" she asked.

Hah, my chance to send her back to her original seat. "I'm a nurse, I said. "I worked in a clinic for children with parasites, malaria, leprosy, all kinds of tropical diseases. In a village that has no other medical resources, you treat whatever someone needs, whatever age, whatever happens to them." *I got drawn into reminiscing.* "You should have seen them riding around on buffalo, naked as jay birds, big wide white-toothed smiles. By the time they were twenty-five though, all those lovely teeth were gone or black from chewing betel nut, their opium.

"Oh, weren't you afraid of catching leprosy? she asked.

"No, you don't catch it easily. I'm healthy and most of the people were more often sick from other things than from leprosy. I didn't know that when I first went there of course, but I got rid of my fears pretty quickly when I felt so needed."

"It sounds like you miss the Thai people," said Tillie. "Do you plan to return soon?

"No, or at least I should say, I don't know," I told her honestly. "I'll be visiting my friend who lives in Seaside for awhile, then make up my mind."

"Then, back you go to Oklahoma, I guess," she said.

"No, I don't have anybody in Oklahoma any more," I answered honestly.

I had already gotten more involved with Tillie than I had intended but she was a listening ear and I hadn't had one of those who could respond so totally in my own language for a long time.

The growing isolation I was beginning to feel in Thailand was one of the reasons I had been losing control of my emotions. That and the absence of beauty. Oh, there was beauty in our village, but the beauty was in the people, in their joyfulness and their sadness and in the way they could be joyful even when they were heartbroken. I wasn't finding beauty in the scorched earth the constant plague of mosquitoes, the bony cattle, the lack of bathing facilities and toilets, the hookworm. And I, an artist, was hearing the call of Monet's lily pads and my own brush and canvas.

Tillie broke into my reverie. "Then where will you go? You don't have anyone in Oklahoma and you don't know if you want to go back to Thailand and you don't know anything about Seaside. I think you're confused. You should find a good woman and settle down. You're still young. Don't know if you'll find a wife young enough to have babies with but we don't need any more of them rug rats in this world anyway. You're a nurse. You and a good wife can take care of other people's babies."

She had hit several rocks and hard places that I didn't want to explore with her right now. "Tillie, I really need to sleep a bit. Do you mind if we don't talk for a little while?"

"Hope I didn't hurt your feelings," Tillie said. "No, I'll be quiet for awhile. If you get hungry, just wake up. I'll buy something for both of us. I'll be quiet now. By the way, what's your real name now that you're back to your real life? I don't think you want to be called Suung anymore."

"My name is Aubrey. And by the way Tillie, the life I've been living is my real life."

She had put me too much at my ease. When I fell asleep my head dropped onto her shoulder. I think that was when she saw her next victim.

CHAPTER 4

We're in Seaside," I heard a quiet voice say. Tillie shook my head roughly with her hunk of a hand. I awoke suddenly. After a dizzying confused moment I noticed the black shiny rim of a skycap's cap move past the window. Oh yes, I was on a train. I shivered. Even though I had taken my arms out of my windbreaker and put it over me like a throw, I was chilled. I hadn't been prepared for forty-degree weather. It was only sixty even in this stuffy coach. It took me another minute to realize that the bump under my head was the shoulder of a stranger, not a pillow. Boy, this was uncomfortable, embarrassing, sleeping on the shoulder of a stranger.

"Oh, I'm sorry. I didn't mean to…" I didn't know what else to say.

She snickered then smiled, showing her row of almost perfect white teeth. She reached over to straighten my shoulders laying her breasts on my chest while doing so. It might have been accidental, even helpful, but it made me uneasy…and now I was thoroughly awake.

"Tillie was your name, wasn't it?" I asked her. I stretched, stood half way and moved past her to the aisle. I grabbed Tillie's duffel bag with my left hand and my own roller bag from the overhead bin with my right.

"I'll carry your bag out for you. Is anyone meeting you?" I asked her. I really wanted to be done with her.

Here I was in Seaside, Oregon. Just outside my window someplace was Cecily and a whole new mystery of a life for me and I was stuck with Tillie. Tillie's voice was mute almost, like far away, because I had zoned her out, already erased her from my life as much as I could.

"No, no one's here to meet me," she said, "but thanks for carrying my bag. I'll just find a taxi."

I thought she'd be gone, but of course she couldn't leave, I was still holding her duffel bag, while I searched the crowd for Cecily. Though Cecily and I had kept in touch regularly by email we had rarely bothered with pictures of ourselves. Sometimes I would send her a picture of the children at the clinic wearing some clothing she had sent to me for them, or she would send me a picture she had taken from her home, of the sunset over the Pacific. It had been so long since we had seen each other face to face that I wasn't sure I would recognize her right away, but when I saw her blond bobbed hair blowing in the wind as she ran toward me I knew Cecily as if I had seen her yesterday.

"Cecily," I yelled as she, with just as much assurance called, "Aubrey." I had been holding Tillie's suitcase as well as my own. I dropped them both at my sides when I saw Cecily. We landed on each other with a bear hug a minute long it seemed, for every year we had been apart. I grabbed her two shoulders and held her at arms length to get the best possible view of this angel. Cecily was dressed in dark blue jeans that were pressed, actually had creases, a white turtle neck sweater, navy sport coat with a red silk pocket handkerchief, tiny diamond earrings, black shoes with Cuban heels. Perfect. I in shorts with the arms of a black windbreaker tied around my waist, looked totally out of place, I'm sure. Tillie stood back watching, totally surprised, I think, to see that the friend I was meeting was a woman. Cecily looking over my shoulder noticed her watching and looked at me questioningly.

"Oh, I'm sorry. Cecily, this is Tillie. She sat next to me on the train and unfortunately for her, had to carry my sleeping head part of the way."

After they greeted each other Tillie offered, "I'll call a cab. The cabbie can see you to your house first and then drop me off."

"No, I have my Ram, but thank you Tillie," Cecily said. "Do you need a lift somewhere?" I winced, moving back from Tillie's line of vision and shaking my head, 'no!' Cecily caught the head shake but apparently missed the message that I didn't want to encourage further association with Tillie.

"Oh, never mind. I'm sure you have your own arrangements. But here, take my card in case you want to get in touch with Aubrey," she said, handing Tillie her business card. Tillie followed us to Cecily's truck. I felt like I was being rude to her, seeing her stand there watching us, like we should offer again to take her, but I loaded my case into the bed of the truck, jumped in the passenger seat and pulled the door shut with a bang. We left her watching us as we drove away.

The sun was shining in Seaside and Cecily had a plan. "The town of Seaside is laid out along a beach of the Pacific Ocean," she explained. "Ocean Blvd parallels the beach."

She drove northward along the sea's edge so that I could be taken in by the massive beach where the sand sparkled in the sunshine. Then she turned right off the boulevard into this quaint town, past the tee shirt and bathing suit shops where the sun flickered on the pastel walls, through trendy Talbot's and Target area and into upscale Brooks Brothers and Neiman's. The prize was yet to come after we returned to the beach and headed to the historic district with Inns and Museums. By now the sun was low over the Pacific Ocean turning the white Tillamook Rock Lighthouse into a yellow, orange and red tower.

"I want you to get a good look at your new home town on a beautiful day," Cecily said excitedly. "It's been grey for too long. One never knows about the weather here. It might be grey again tomorrow. This fifty degrees is pleasant when the sun is shining but wait til June. It's gorgeous here. I know its not hot like Thailand, but you'll get used to it again, I mean, used to living in a cold climate for a part of the year. The weather helps mark the years as they go by too fast. This town shuts down completely after dark especially in winter. I know it also seems pretty empty now even though it's not dark yet."

"Cecily, this town does not seem empty to me. Where I've come from there's no such thing as a street light and no electricity in the houses yet. Dark there is really dark, when the moon isn't full and the stars aren't sparkling. And my village has only dirt paths, no roads, no businesses, so people are all home after dark."

Cecily seemed to be assuming that I was moving in with her forever. Me, I was just perplexed. I had no idea what was next other than a search for a new life. Would I consider Oklahoma again, after having grown up on a farm? Sure, I could be comfortable there again, but not alone. What were my options? With no family there in Oklahoma, old friends were all living their own lives now. Well maybe I'd take a trip there sometime and get the feel of farm life again.

Then there was Thailand. I could still feel Thailand. Maybe that would end up being my forever home after all. Besides all that, I haven't accumulated any money yet. There was no fortune to be made in Muang Iai. I would need a job someplace and soon. In Muang Iai I earned forty dollars a month like the local people, plus housing. Of course, there was no place to spend my money either, so I got along just fine on my forty.

And Seaside? So far it just seems like a vacation place. I won't be happy being on vacation the rest of my life.

"You're quiet Aubrey. Thinking? Do you like what you see? Cecily asked.

"It's beautiful, Cecily," I responded. "But then, there are a lot of beautiful places. I have to find my fit. I'm just dreaming right now…could this be it?"

"Hey, tell me about this Tillie that you just shared your ride and your head with. There obviously was some reason you didn't want her to ride along with us just now. She seemed to me like a pretty nice gal, though weird. She sure seemed to like you."

"Cecily, I don't know her at all. First of all she was only the woman that happened to be sitting next to me, not someone I chose or want to associate with. Also I thought she was too familiar for a stranger. It made me uncomfortable. I was really embarrassed when I woke up with my head on her shoulder. Anyway, a woman in my life right now is the last thing I need. First I have to figure out what I want in life before I start dealing with what somebody else wants."

"Smart, Aubrey. What do you plan to do with this wonderful gift of life?" She asked.

"Yes, what do I plan to do with this wonderful life?" I mused.

Cecily waited.

"This great adventurous life you mean? I hope to be delighted with this life Cecily, in time. That's about as much as I can envision right now. And of course, getting a job is first order. What do you think the job potential is for me in Seaside?"

Cecily answered the same thing everybody always says: "Nurses can always get a job, there are so many places a nurse can work."

"So what do you mean by Tillie being 'too familiar'," she asked after some thought.

"Well, she moved from her original seat to sit by me uninvited. I wanted to be alone so that I'd have the answers to all your questions by the time I got here. Then she let me sleep on her shoulder. She could have moved me when I fell on her instead of waiting for the whole trip to wake me. She got kind of too cozy, I think. Then she wanted to come home with us."

"I think you just have to get used to United States Americans again, Aubrey. We are a casual people and make friends easily. Besides, what's there not to be attracted to when she saw you sitting alone? You're like a woman magnet," Cecily said.

Aubrey let that frightening thought sink in.

"What do you want to do first now that you're here?" Cecily asked. "Should we stop someplace for coffee?"

"First, I just want to get to your house. I'm dying to get 'home' get warm, put my feet up, then…"

I knew what I needed most so I interrupted myself, "First talk. Then talk some more. Then see your house and have dinner and maybe talk some more. Then, I desperately need clothes so tomorrow I must shop but we can talk some more too."

"The next question, what do you want to eat tonight?"

"Anything that I can chew, like a steak or pork chop and potatoes and ice cream. I've had nothing but rice and cut up things and dessert made from rice for about eight years," I told her.

Finally, Cecily turned left into the driveway of a small house on the big beach.
"We're home!" she said.

I sat quietly for an eternal thirty seconds observing her little home on the beach, wondering what life here was like

Here we were at Cecily's house where I would be staying probably for just a little while. The neighboring houses both north and south of Cecily's were about half a block away so she had a long stretch of beach to herself. All the nearby houses like hers were one story ranch houses. On the beach side of this house was a large yard with a sand colored wrought iron fence around it to keep Romeo, her canine lord of the manor, from frightening beach goers when he was out sun bathing. Her front porch on the street side had a red plaid two-seater swing hanging by a chain. She had kept her light turned on even in the bright sunlight to welcome me. The only green lawn was between her garage door driveway and front porch, a necessity, she said, so that she wouldn't drag too much sand into the house every time she comes home.

Here it was, my nearest future, the place that Cecily had described to me as 'perfect for two'. The two turned out to have six legs between them, legs of Cecily and Romeo, her dog.

How many times would I walk in this front door? Would I work here? Fall in love here? Or feel an urgency to get away to somewhere else from here? Beginning anew would mean changing my mind and heart, not just my location. I would be finding a new way of life. If I had fond memories of my past in Thailand, I would become a new me here in Oregon and I was determined to love my future wherever it would be.

My reverie was interrupted by "woof, woof".

Romeo Cecily's black Doberman, with full-length ears and tail, no clipping a dog for her, greeted us politely at the front door. I stood there feeling strangely excited but hesitant to enter, until Romeo ran around behind me and nudged me forward. He followed me with his nose touching my legs as if he had always been my dog as we walked room to room through her house.

Most of the house had pinkish sand color tile floors, easier to sweep up or hide the sand, she said. The rooms were bright enough that the chocolate colored walls in the bedrooms didn't darken them. She had hung bright paintings that picked up the sunlight, like red, white and green bird of paradise flowers in her bedroom. On a small table in her bedroom she kept an old dollhouse. It was turned facing the wall so that you could see all the small furnishings she had collected over the years through its open backside.

Cecily showed me into the guest bedroom with pride. "Your room." It was about 14 x 14 but with windows all along it on the beach side. I had my own closet with space for a dozen times the amount of my belongings and my own bathroom with a pocket door between the two rooms. Except for a bright multicolored, almost gaudy quilt on the bed, it was decorated with pink and turquoise paintings, a little too feminine for me but then, as a beggar, you can't be, well, you know the rest of it. When I decided where to live long-term I could decorate my own space with muscle, macho stuff.

  The kitchen was small but had room for a square wooden table and chairs in the middle. The cabinets were wooden, matching the table, a light colored maple. The walls were yellow and the appliances white. The ocean facing French windows had white and yellow café curtains pulled back for a full view of the water. On the kitchen window sill stood a child's teapot and cup set. This cozy warm kitchen aroused in me the feeling of finally being home, of being welcomed to my own home. It felt like when you smell biscuits just taken from an oven or like seeing your mother smiling from behind her apron.

  Cecily had anticipated what I would want to eat. She had bought just the right things for my first dinner. It was fun for me helping her cook a real American dinner, though I should say watching her rather than helping. She creamed the carrots and peas, stuffed a pork roast and glazed sweet potatoes. I was immensely enjoying the aroma of American cooking while she was laughing at my ignorance of modern conveniences like her digital meat thermometer and the air pressure cork remover she told me to use to get that darn cork out of the wine bottle.

We ate our first dinner together at Cecily's eat-in kitchen table. We washed and dried dishes together. Cecily excused herself while she changed into jeans and gave me time to unpack my one bag. By the time we both came back to the living room she had a fire started in the wood burning fireplace and was comfortably seated, feet up waiting for me.

CHAPTER 5

Cecily's living room was brightened by the log fire and wall sconces. The sun had fallen below the edge of the Pacific now leaving the room with a dim glow. The floor of the room was light wide-board maple and softened by a round bright colored braided rag rug. Her two-seater recliner and three other comfortable chairs picked up the colors in the rug and the red and yellow of the fireplace flame. On the wall over the fireplace Cecily had hung a rectangular painting of her parents' wheatfield in Oklahoma, that I painted for her years ago. Cecily's home was neat and uncluttered but instead of knickknacks she had placed old toys, probably from her own childhood, a sock-doll on her book case, a doll cradle angled in one corner of the living room, a toy fire engine on the fireplace mantle. She was keeping her memories warm, I thought. She must miss her home very much.

When we retired to the living room after dinner Romeo sat on his big cushion by the fireplace, his head or eyes turning from one of us to the other as we spoke, apparently understanding every word.

"Do you have lots of pictures of your village? Cecily asked. I can't wait to see them. You obviously didn't bring any of your paintings in your little bag."

I pulled out my pink and yellow pasin and told Cecily its story. "I didn't bring many pictures though," I told her. "I was going to say 'not much to photograph', but to be honest, it's a bad excuse. There were thousands of subjects. I just forgot about taking pictures once I got on with life there.

It was beautiful in my Thai village, but it wasn't exactly the kind of beauty to take pictures of or paint. The people were so poor. They searched the clinic garbage dump for little white bugs to eat. Sometimes that was their only protein, though some had chickens giving them eggs to eat and to use for bartering. People walked miles, even days to come to our clinic and they were so hot and dirty when they got there. Then they sat on the ground outside the clinic waiting their turn to be seen. Sometimes they waited even overnight.

They brought little tins of rice to have food for the journey and drank water from the klong, that's the water that stands on the side of the road where buffalo and bicycles are washed and jute is dyed. Can you believe it? That was drinking water for them. After we treated their foot ulcers or their fever we had to send them walking back home all that way in ninety degree heat. They'd be carrying a little medicine or bandages or whatever we had that they needed. That's why they liked injections so much. The results lasted longer. If we had slow-release injectable medicine available we always used that since we didn't have refills available. I'm sure that by the time they got home they were more sick than before they came."

"Aubrey, why did you stay in Thailand so long when you felt so helpless?"

"You remember, I thought it would be an adventure filling in for the long-time nurse while she came back to the States for a few months. When she didn't return I just couldn't leave those people without even one nurse. Then before I found a replacement for myself, my parents were killed…"

It all came flooding back, a torrent of emotions pounding on my heart, hurting in my chest. I had buried these emotions along with my parents. I started to think about them again. Silence fell between us as Cecily allowed me to finally feel my sadness.

"They must have been driving along, enjoying each other, who knows, maybe even talking about me and my latest letter. Then suddenly, Boom! They never even knew what happened, the cops said." They died on impact, their little convertible versus an eighteen wheeler. They didn't stand a chance. I don't really know why they were in their convertible. They usually towed it behind their motor home on these trips, but that time they left without the motor home. Maybe they were just going for a joy ride, who knows?

"Do you suppose they were distracted?" Cecily asked.

"Not by a cell phone for sure. My Dad never used the phone when he was driving. I hope it was an easy ending for them but it was a shocking and sad ending for their son."

"I was numb for a long time after that. I kept working, never came home for the funeral. Why should I? There was no one in Oklahoma who needed me. I decided that I was fortunate to have my hard work to distract me. And living among people who had so little compared to me just made me grateful for the years I'd had my parents. I never properly grieved though, never had anyone to hug or cry with, just went right back to work. Maybe I have to take a trip to Oklahoma sometime just to do that, to grieve, to see all the things that were dear to them. Maybe walking on the farm, visiting whoever is now in our house, a Sunday morning at our church would help me grieve. Maybe that's what is keeping me from feeling close to anyone.

"Cecily, I am so grateful that you were able to go to my parents' funeral for me. There was really no one there that needed me and I could not have made it on time for their service anyway. As you remember, it was all preplanned. They were to be cremated immediately and have Reverend Janice perform their funeral service within a week. They had been traveling constantly for years. They were well aware that they could be in an accident together sometime so they didn't want the problem of arrangements to be left for me. And their stuff? There wasn't much of that any more. Uncle Oscar took care of that and the camper they lived in."

Cecily wanted me to know that she relished the memory of that time with my family and that representing me had not been a burden for her.

"Your uncle Oscar!" she recalled, "What a guy! Puffing on that cigar, his gruff voice, yeah, he sounded like Louie Armstrong, 'Hey Cec, take some of this stuff here. Sure you can use some o this stuff.' I couldn't carry anything large on the plane of course. None of it was worth the cost of shipping.

"Did you recognize the handmade quilt on your bed? She continued. "That's yours Aubrey. That's the one thing of your Mom's I managed to bring back for you, that and the box of paints that were your Dad's. And Aubrey, I can hear your Dad say, 'Don't mourn too long for us Aubrey. Keep having a good life. We are both so happy we had you, got to watch you grow up into a gentleman, we're so proud of you.'"

We sat and watched the fire for a long time while I thought contentedly and so sadly of my parents pride in me. While my tears found the channels on my face that had been used before, I moved over by Romeo and sat down beside him. I scratched him under the ears and his tail wagged ever so slightly, letting me know he was trying to understand. What would I do now to honor my parents? Cecily laid her head back on the recliner smiling while she remembered my uncle Oscar. Romeo dozed off warmed by the still red hot coals in the fireplace.

Cecily finally broke the silence. "I think one of the things that binds us so closely is that we're both only children. For good or for bad, that made us different than our other friends. There was no one for you to go home to when your parents died. That is very sad. Your parents were the greatest. Even though you were the only child that they had, they gave you your freedom when the time came for you to leave home and become a professional adventurer. You could do what you needed to do. If they knew they were going to die when they did, they still would have wanted you to stay in Thailand and be with those people who did need you.

"Going to their funeral was the least I could do for you. I couldn't cry with the same feeling you would have had, but I could be a person for the friends of your parents to hug, feeling that it was like a way to hug you. Your parents had many friends and everyone I spoke with seemed to understand why you weren't there and they were happy that I came," she said.

Then she had to add, "Nobody even called me a honky."

"Do you think one gets used to being lonely when you're a kid?" I asked.

"I didn't know I was lonely, it's just the way it was. I had parents at home and friends outside of home. I think now though, that loneliness was the main reason I ended up getting pregnant so young. I needed someone to be close to, not just my parents, but a peer to replace the sibling thing. Boy, did that backfire," After musing on that a bit she said, "Despite my situation, pregnancy was a powerful, beautiful experience for me. Every day when I was pregnant I would wake up and look at my stomach and think, 'another person, right here with me.'"

"Are you in touch with your parents now, Cecily?" I asked her.

"Only superficially. We send each other Christmas and birthday cards. We email when there's something important like a new address or job. But the really important things, like Bobby, nope, not a word passes between us, no phone calls, no emails or text," Cecily said belligerently.

"You still think a lot about Bobby, don't you. Do you know where he is or anything about him?" I asked

"He is twenty years old now. I'll never know and always know. I think of him every day. It seemed like I could hear him playing on the street when he was three and worried he'd be hit by a car. I heard the sound of his voice changing to a low pitch when he was thirteen. I just knew I was hearing him as valedictorian when he was eighteen. Yet I know nothing about him. I don't know if he is blond or brunette. If he rang my doorbell right now I'd answer the door and ask, 'are you the young man who is coming to mow my lawn?' And he would have to shyly to tell me that he is my son.

"When my parents sent me to Portland to stay with an aunt until the baby was born I fully intended to keep him. I was only sixteen. When they tricked me into giving him up I determined that they would know what it feels like to lose a child. It just couldn't end this way, a beautiful little boy that I breast fed one time and wanted to protect forever. And he was gone. After that, I could never return to my parents' home. I'd rather be alone than go back to them. The only thing strong enough to teach them, about the pain their lies caused me, is for them to experience losing a child. So, they've lost me."

"Cecily, people do the best they can. I think your parents did their best. Their experience was, that a young girl needs to finish her education in order to get along in this world. Years ago, it wasn't possible for a girl with a baby to continue high school most places. It had to be kept a big secret when a girl got pregnant. Course, we guys were home free when that happened. That doesn't mean it was okay for them to deceive you. But maybe someday you can have compassion for them, for the bad choices they made," I said.

"I don't see how," she said.

Cecily continued, "I stayed with my aunt til after high school and I found this messenger job in Seaside and went to night school for college, in Portland. When you were taking that course in anthropology for fun, I was taking it to work on a degree, staying in a raunchy motel and working two jobs so that some day I could have a better job, a better future. And I've done it. I love Seaside so I probably will not move to a bigger city to make more money. I have enough now to support my independence. I own my own travel and real estate agencies, life is good for me here."

"Your own plum trees and a home on the beach," I said.

"Yeah, plums and a beach. Not a bad life if you can't afford a castle and a butler and a chef of your own to cook the meat and potatoes" Cecily responded.

Cecily said, "Don't forget I stayed with you after you discovered my raunchy motel. That was a blast. Do you remember that summer night when we were headed to 'The Garden'. You told me it was a monastery garden. I dressed all proper, calf length skirt, even brought a white lace veil in my purse, and it turned out to be a beer garden. Mario Lanza-type beer garden with picnic tables surrounded by ivy. Every time a new bunch of people came in they sat down and started to sing The Drink Song. We could tell what was coming when one of the guys would lift a girl up onto the table.

"Do you keep up with any of our friends from those days, Cecily?" I asked.

She thought about it. "I did for awhile but my life was so different from theirs. I never did make close friends there between working and school. We gradually just didn't have much in common.

"Now about you Aubrey, let's talk about you, how are you feeling about all the changes you're going through right now? About Seaside, about living with me, about looking for work?"

"Oh God, Cecily, I feel so disconnected. It's not just the job, it's life. I don't have time or energy or even an excuse for self-pity. I've had such a good life and here you are, such a good friend. But I still want, have always wanted a wife and family and home of my own. I've escaped the search for so long. When you're young you think it will just happen. But if it doesn't just happen, then what? That's where I am now."

"Do you even know what kind of job to hunt for?"

"I'll peruse the papers and ads. I'll check all the medical facilities and set up interviews. I need to start with nursing jobs because that's my education and experience. Fortunately I'm a nurse. There's almost always some kind of job for a nurse, as you said. But I could probably be happy painting or being a handyman if that's what turns up for me. For all I know now, I might end up going back to the Thai village where I know I was useful. But before I do that I have to find out if that's really where I want to be for the rest of my life. I can't expect to start over again when I'm fifty or sixty. It's now or never."

Cecily didn't say anything.

"When I tell people about my job or my experience they inevitably say something the equivalent of 'aren't you wonderful'. But you know Cecily, I figure it's just as wonderful to contribute to someone's vacation or to make someone laugh or to be a scientist, discover stars, or to be a parent, discover a child's perspective. It takes us all together to make the world go round. I'm tired of being a hero. I can't remember the last time I laughed hard enough to shake my guts."

She didn't say anything.

"If I'm not too much in your way, I'd like to job hunt before I move out of your house. Then I'll have money to buy or rent something around here. I don't really know where I want to end up but Seaside is the best place I can think of to get a start."

Silence.

"Cecily, say something."

"Oh, Aubrey, you need to laugh. I'm not exactly a comedian but...I'd be so excited if you could set up life in Seaside. I'll help you settle in and find a job and some friends and an apartment but you're the one who needs to find you again.

"Who ever would have guessed that in our middle age we'd both be single and both be in Seaside? Life is not what you plan is it? I mean, looking backward we both have amazing stories we could never have planned. But looking forward? Who knows?"

"We have to make our own stories."

"I have great expectations for you Aubrey."

"Don't."

Romeo was dreaming of something scary, of some chase he was about to embark on. He growled ferociously in his sleep, then a log shifted in the fireplace and woke him. He jumped up ready to attack it. He had to be always ready for the kill. Maybe he knew something we didn't know.

CHAPTER 6

I **shouldn't have been worried** about getting settled in Seaside. It all worked out better than I could have planned. The day after my arrival in Seaside I went shopping with Cecily showing me the best places. She had taken the week off from her work to get me settled. We about emptied the medium-size racks in the men's stores and in Target and the whole town was out of size ten shoes by the time we finished. Next I needed a walking tour of this humongous town.

The town of Seaside is a gleaming sun kissed mix of storybook past and modern beach town present. In the 1870s it sported a home, the Ben Holladay Villa, built in 1871 on what is now The Gearhart Links. It is famous for its wooden boardwalk, a promenade now called Lewis and Clark Way. The city Mothers and Fathers must have done a good job of drawing tourists who stayed, because it now has a population of about 6,500 and has grown 22% since the year 2000.

The Salt Works of Seaside commemorate the arrival of Lewis and Clark here on the west coast. This is where they landed after their long trek across the wilderness of a young United States of

America. Salt was vital to their expedition for food preservation and I guess they used it all up. They would need more for the return trip, so they set up camp here at the foot of the sand dunes where they could garnish it from the sea and dry it out in the sun. Here they also bartered for blubber and oil.

"Grandest and most pleasing prospect which my eyes ever surveyed." This is what Clark had said of the environs of the Tillamook Lighthouse. He continued, "In my front, a boundless Ocean…the Seas brake with great force and give the Coast a most romantic appearance."

After Cecily went back to work I took a week to contemplate my future and myself. It seemed like I had the best start in a new life that one could imagine. This was an interesting small town that would be easy for me to negotiate after my long time out of the country. It had several health care facilities, hopefully with employment opportunities and best of all I had here a good friend at this time in my life when I needed one so badly.

Sitting here in the sun facing the "boundless ocean with romantic appearance," through Cecily's glass doors, it was a little hard for me to face job-hunting, but I decided against her protests that it was time.

So on my third Monday morning in the United States, I dressed in a navy blue suit, the Italian cut that fit me perfectly without tailoring, white shirt, red, blue and white tie and black oxfords. I had a fresh short hair cut which was the shortest length that dog groomers show on their length guide. It squared off my forehead and the beautician said, "showed off my dimples". I did not have any earrings, nose or ear piercing or tattoos. I think I looked confident and professional.

My recent experience, eight years of it, could not be called "similar experience" for any job, so I started my search with facilities that boasted care of the elderly, at least educationally appropriate for me. I had with me a list of medical facilities. Providence Seaside Hospital with a Memory Care Unit was first on my list, then Seaside Rehabilitation and Therapy Center, then four Assisted Living facilities. Providence was first so I made a nine o'clock appointment with a manager at Providence. I made no further appointments, not knowing if or how long I'd be at the first one.

Cecily dropped me off two blocks from the hospital so that I could walk east on Wahanna Road to the hospital and get acquainted with the hospital's surroundings. The hospital was in the older part of town among the historical sites, near the Gilbert Inn. It had a new addition but the old part had been designated for the Memory Care Unit in which I was interested. It was a more pleasing, graceful and warm home for "heaven's door" than the new section. It was graced with French windows and doors, warm maple woodwork and even some flowered wallpaper in the bedrooms that would be familiar to the older residents. The entrance to the Memory Care Unit was bordered with purple petunias. A large safe-walk between the newer building and the older section, had an ocean view and allowed residents space to amble without fear of getting lost and to sit on benches and have important discussions with each other and with with staff.

Cecily had warned me that although I was well qualified with a master's degree in geriatric nursing, there were almost no people of color in Seaside. My interviewers might be taken by surprise when they met me in person. Although she said, she had found this town very inviting, I might not have the same experience. Always good to be prepared for the worst, she had said, then be pleasantly surprised by the best. I remembered my parents gratefully as I approached this interview. They had taught me the pride and dignity, that enabled me to present myself and my experience and talents with self-confidence.

The other problem I foresaw with gaining employment was an eight-year absence of a job reference. I brought a few pictures of me with the kids in the clinic to show that I was really there. I had a reference from the Church that had hired my predecessor and myself in Thailand, and paid our salary of forty dollars a month in American money during the whole ten years of our work there. This reference, however, was not a professional nursing reference. It didn't prove continuity of employment. Brother Philip could speak for my integrity, hard work, reliability and caring but might not be able to speak for my nursing outcomes, the professional jargon that might be needed for employment in the United States. Outcomes? We considered ourselves blessed if we could send someone back to their shack a little more able to drive the bicycle that pulled their tuk tuk than they had been during their illness. That was my measure of outcome, not lack of infection and rate of recidivism, the measures used here in the United States.

I was right in time for my interview and was led directly into the office of Dr. Geary, the Medical Officer in Charge and also Administrator of the facility. Fifty year old Dr. Seamus Geary was gracious and a natural extrovert. He dressed like a man who had a wife to check each morning to see that his tie matched his socks, though I understand that he had never been married. He was dressed now, all business, navy double breasted suit with brass buttons, leather shoes, white shirt and he 'shot -the-cuff to display golden cufflinks when he straightened his orange tie. His appearance belied the inner Seamus Geary, whose eyes twinkled with his ready laugh. In the corner of the office I noticed also, a pair of jeans and golf shirt hanging from a coat tree. He apparently was not all business.

On the walls of his office, hung numerous degrees and diplomas. One showed that he had completed a residency in Ophthalmic Surgery at Jules Stein Eye Institute of UCLA in the year 2,000. I wondered why he had given up the practice of eye surgery in favor of hospital administration. He seemed like a man who would want to be with patients, not paper work.

He stood when I entered the office and reached over to shake hands with me. He came around from behind his mahogany desk and motioned for me to sit on the brown leather sofa across the room, positioned for the ocean view it provided. He rang his secretary and without questioning me, asked her to bring the tray which supplied coffee, cream, sugar, tea and one-bite cookies. He was genuinely interested in my experience in Thailand. I didn't need to worry about producing evidence of my employment. The enthusiasm I couldn't hide when I described my work was evidence enough, he said. He had personal experience with, and appreciation for my situation. I learned from him that he himself had worked in Pago Pago, American Samoa for several years as a volunteer with "Doctors Without Borders."

By the end of my interview I had a potential job. It was such a perfect job for me that I didn't need to pursue the other facilities but I did anyway. After I was employed at Providence I found that it helped me in my job, to have met the owners and managers of these other facilities. I often had business dealings with them when a resident was being transferred between facilities. As a result of these original 'getting to know you' interviews, I initiated quarterly meetings of all the managers of senior care facilities in the area. Even when there were no problems for them to resolve, the meetings turned out to be a great support system for people in a similar difficult profession.

When my day was done, I went back to Cecily's to await a phone call hoping to set up further interviews at Providence.

The four interviews I endured there all went smoothly. I met with the Administrators for Nursing, for Human Resources, for Trauma and Emergency Care and for Financial Management. Race was never mentioned except by Dr. Geary who said, "it will sure be good for all of us to have somebody a little different around here." He may have been referring to my international experience rather than to the fact that I'm a male black master degreed nurse, I persuaded myself. I wasn't convinced that this was my forever future but I was sure that I would stay here long enough to reward the confidence the managers had placed in me. I already had plans for making this the country's best Memory Care Unit.

By the next week I was the manager of both the sixty bed Memory Care Unit and the Rehabilitation Unit at Providence Seaside Hospital. My orientation and salary would begin in one week. Everything was falling into place so perfectly. Cecily and I agreed that it would be best for me to live with her for a while longer both for the company that we provided for each other and to allow my bank account to build a little before I started looking for another place to live. We also agreed to tell each other clearly when we felt it was time to move on, for her to kick me out or for me to scoot.

Sitting before the fire with Romeo that night, we had the elephant in the living room conversation.

"Aubrey, this is hard for me to bring up," she started. Cecily didn't want me to think that she wanted me to leave. "Have you ever thought of me in romantic terms? I mean, did you ever think of sleeping with me?"

I had to laugh. Amazingly, we had never had this conversation. "Of course I thought of it. What do you think I am, a brick? I think of it every day, but I would never ask you for that."

"Why are you laughing?" she asked.

"Because," I said.

"Because what? Am I that unattractive to you?" she quizzed.

"Of course not," I said. "It's just that I have wondered why you never married and I didn't want to ask. I was thinking you should be hooking up with somebody. But I was thinking of somebody else, not with me. You know how much we enjoy each other, but, well, we're like brother and sister. It would almost seem like incest to marry you. We'd be a great pair, you wanting to stay put forever and me restless to go. Anyway, as of now, it just ain't happenin. I'm so glad of that."

"Whew," then Cecily laughed too. "So Bro, we better have a beer and drink to the best friend one could ever have."

Cecily was still not convinced that we had closed the deal. Maybe she had been hoping. She waited, then said thoughtfully, "Promise me that if romance ever becomes an issue while you're living here we move you out instantly. We wouldn't want to muddy the waters. Then we could date seriously and without any pressure or ambivalence…without the flutter, til we're both ready for it."

Holding my right arm up to the sky I said, "I solemnly swear and promise."

I went to the refrigerator and brought back two Ice cold bottles of Sam Adams. We giggled like kids, and clinked bottles, "to best friends ever," she said.

"And to great sex with somebody else," I added.

"You know, your neighbors probably figured out the first day I was here that we're some kind of couple, either an unseemly affair…"

"Or something seamy or steamy," she finished for me.

"To neighbors," I said, and we clinked again.

Such a smooth and happy beginning of my new life Stateside had to be a portent of a pleasant life ahead of me. It was always a pleasure to come home after work to share the kitchen, a glass of wine and our stories, then to allow each other privacy while preparing for the next day. But why did I still have this feeling of looking into the unknown, like I was sitting on the rocks dangling my feet in the water but the water was too cold or to rough. I was not yet ready to dive in, even to wade, for pete's sake.

CHAPTER 7

***"H*ey Aubrey, let me show you something,"** she said. "This is what I call 'dating online' or better, 'risk free dating'. You just sign on with this dating site. You will be given a whole list of women you can 'date online'. You can choose interesting people who live far away so that they know you're not looking for a real date or a sleepover. Then you can have fun conversations with great looking women. At least you think they're great looking. You never know for sure if the picture you get from them on line is really their picture or the story they're telling is really their story. That's the good part. That way, you can also fake your own story if you want to. You know, tit for tat."

"Why bother, if you're not really looking for an honest relationship?" I asked.

"People do it all the time. It's just for fun," Cecily said.

"Okay, lets see. I'm a strawberry blond (whose picture can I use for that?) age twenty and I'm in nursing school in San Francisco. Is that what you mean?" I asked.

"Well not exactly," Cecily said. "You'd probably want to use your own picture, but it can be an old one so you look younger. I

Flowering

wouldn't give anyone my real address and phone number but I'd want to use my real hometown and age in order to get a response that's really interesting. It probably wouldn't be fun to carry on a lengthy relationship, even online with an eighteen year old from Portland who's wanting to date you or with a seventy year old who was just widowed. But a thirty year old from New York or even Thailand would be fun."

"I don't get it Cecily," I said. "I'd have to make a choice. Either I really want a genuine relationship and I tell the truth or I just want to play games, in which case anyone can be fun, seventeen or seventy, student or widow."

So I decided, why not try it? Creativity out the door. I wrote about the real me. Three days later I checked my computer. "Oh my God Cecily, I already have eight responses and I used my true self picture wearing my work suit, tie and all. Can you believe that eight women would be interested in me? I didn't give your address or even a phone number like you suggested. Here's what I said. I read it to her.

I'm thirty-six years young, five feet, ten inches tall.
I have real short hair parted on the left side. I have a long
shaped face to match my long lean body and broad
shoulders.

I have oodles of energy and I'm pretty smart. My college

> *degrees are in nursing and philosophy with a masters degree in geriatric nursing but art is really my first love. My friends say that I'm good looking in color, they couldn't imagine me in white. I'm the manager of Memory Care and Rehabilitation units at Providence Hospital in Seaside, Oregon."*

It was a new self-image for me. It felt so strange introducing myself as a manager of a hospital specialty unit from Seaside, Oregon. Every time I wrote or spoke that self-description, I had to stop and think or re-read what I had said.

I chose three of the responses that I had received and wrote a return message to each of them saying that I just got back from eight years in Thailand where I was nursing people with leprosy. I figured that message would get rid of any woman who was just interested in sex games online or who was a romance scam artist looking for a rich bastard to rob. It may have worked.

Only one of those three wrote back this time. Her name was Aida. The name sounded fake enough but I wasn't going to write her off just because of her name. I figured her Mom was probably an opera buff, named her after the opera she liked best. She hadn't asked me any foolish questions like, was I afraid of catching leprosy or was I afraid of snakes. This was her next response.

- - - - - - - - - -

From <aidasadat@icloud.com

To<aubreygentile@hotmail.com

Hi Aubrey, I'm Caucasian, five feet and five inches tall and weigh one hundred and fifteen pounds. "I am Muslim but *I do not wear a hijab, never have. It would really be in the way, be dirty all the time with my gardening work and all. I usually wear my hair in a French braid that reaches to my scapula. I'm a landscape artist. I'm also thirty-six years old, never married. I live in Copperhill, Tennessee which is a tiny depressed town of about 350 people. I work full time for the city of Blue Ridge, Georgia designing and landscaping their main drag and I work part time independently. Interesting about your experience in Thailand. My mom was a nurse. She would have loved doing what you've done because she was full of adventure, but then I came along and ruined her plans for adventure. Tell me more about your work in Thailand.* Sincerely, *Aida Sadat*

In another email Aida said,

- - - - - - - - - -

From <aidasadat@icloud.com

To<aubreygentile@hotmail.com

A wealthy family has bought up a lot of acreage in Copperhill. The rumor is that they plan to rehabilitate this town. That is great news for me and my profession as a lot of landscaping will be needed. So far several new businesses have opened in just the last few months. It looks like the rumors are true.

We started writing about weekly, which quickly became daily.

- - - - - - - - - -

From <aidasadat@icloud.com

To <aubreygentile@hotmail.com

I grew up in a very "ordinary" American life in Nashville, Tennessee, midtown America, even though I was born in Iran. My mother is a nurse, my father was a banker. He died five years ago. I have one brother, Francis, who is two years older than me and a sister Jocelyn, whom I think of as a baby sister that I need to protect, even though we are also only two years apart. Maybe that feeling arose because she was born in this country shortly after we arrived here, and my insecure parents taught me to protect her. But our family adapted quickly to our new country, as both of my parents needed to work, both spoke English and we kids were whisked off to day care. My parents had to take the chance, they had no one else to care for us.

Our fledgling online relationship was developing nicely and was becoming more intimate.

- - - - - - - - - -

From <aidasadat@icloud.com
To<aubreygentile@hotmail.com

"Aubrey, do you want children?"

From<aubreygentile@hotmail.com
To<aidasadat@icloud.com

"I'd like a ton of them." The trouble is I don't want them to have to call me 'gramps'. On the other hand, maturity might make for good parenting. What about you, Aida?"

----

*From<aidasadat@icloud.com
To<aubreygentile@hotmail.com
Me too. And I'd like my children to be every color of the rainbow and have every talent including ordinariness.*

Strangely, online conversations with Aida seemed to be more interesting and fulfilling than those I had with real people around me. I rushed home every day to get in a few minutes of personal computer time with Aida before Cecily arrived, not to exclude Cecily but so that I could concentrate on Aida. I would check several times a day to see if anything had come from Aida. I found it hard to fake my real feelings when I wrote to Aida. If I was jazzed up about something, she knew it and if not she called me on it.

Chapter 8

*T*hen one day Tillie showed up a Cecily's office asking for my contact information.

"Aubrey, I didn't tell her how to call you directly because at the train station you seemed hesitant to keep in touch with her. If I were you, which I'm not, I'd say 'yes' to her. What can it hurt? You don't have any commitment to Aida it seems to me. You really don't seem to want a commitment yet, and Tillie seems like a 'no commitment' kind of a girl. Besides, you need some social life besides me. I'm boring. Maybe you could check out some museum or gala to volunteer for. Or how about a charity or church fund to raise money for. You can meet all kinds of people doing volunteer work."

"Oh, God help me. Even Tillie would be better than volunteering for a church. Once the church finds out they have real live free help it never stops. But about Tillie, I don't want to give her the impression that I'm interested in her romantically. She's so forward."

"That's easy. Just meet her at Finn's Fish House on kids-eat-free night. In all the commotion the kids cause she'll get the message that you're not ready for romance with her," Cecily suggested.

So that was the plan and it worked. Tillie met me outside of Finn's Fish House, took my arm and strutted in with me, seeming to be as proud as a newly groomed poodle. She was dressed like a tourist, white shorts, sandals, black tee and a black and white tweed sport jacket. She looked more slender than she did in the camouflage gear I had seen her in previously. Still no makeup but curly hair neatly combed and pearl earrings. The weather was still a little cool for shorts, but that's what most of the tourists wear here in any weather so it fits in Seaside. I wasn't even embarrassed to be with her.

And she seemed to enjoy the kids. No angry looks or gestures at all their boisterousness. The kid at the next booth to us spilled his chocolate milk and Tillie jumped up to hold the baby while his mother cleaned it up.

After such a good first experience I felt more comfortable asking Tillie out. She often was unavailable, out of town, she said, usually on the train going somewhere. She had great stories to tell about her train rides but was evasive about where she was headed and why.

After several months of hanging out with Tillie I still didn't know where she lived, if she had parents or siblings or who her friends were. I didn't know her age, her educational history or what

Flowering

kind of work she did. I didn't know what movies she liked, what books she read, what she liked to eat or if she had any hobbies. She apparently didn't like to dance because she never suggested meeting at a place where they had dancing. In other words, I didn't know what made her tick. I did know she was a smoker. I knew she had tattoos, a snake on her leg, and a goat on her neck. I had no idea about more intimate or hidden places for a tattoo. Most frequently because of my work and her frequent absence, we hit the local bars rather than planning for dinner, a show or other entertainment. My favorite was the Naked Winery Tasting Room because it was a good place to meet other people. It had stand-up tables and free hors d'oeuvres. Sometimes competition between sturgeon and salmon fishermen would heat up in the bar. The fishermen were so much fun to listen to. They'd all be at the bar in overalls with red wrinkled windburned faces at the tired end of their day. They were jolly even though tired, and kept the mugs of beer coming, happily throwing peanut shells on the bare wooden floor in this restaurant that wasn't a peanut-shell-floor restaurant. The bartenders and wait staff never stopped the peanut thing. Their acceptance was probably good for big tips at the end of the evening.

    I never invited Tillie to Cecily's home despite Cecily's welcome and I never took Tillie home to her place, wherever that was. She often had a rented car, which meant we had two cars with which to return home. When I asked Tillie where she was staying it was always something like,

"I spend most of my time in San Francisco," or "I just use different motels when I'm in Seaside." Despite her initial interest in my nursing experience, she never asked about Thailand or my present job. This did not seem to be a relationship that was going anywhere but I was having fun so it didn't matter to me. When I discussed our "dates" with Cecily she seemed to think it was a little weird, even creepy.

"After all these dates, most people expect to know a little about each other," she said. "If a guy acted like that with me I'd be afraid of him, but then, you men don't seem to have the fear factor like we women do. I just hope you don't fall in love with a woman like that. She's sure not open to you and she doesn't seem concerned that you live with me, a woman and your best friend. Doesn't she ever ask to get together with your friends?"

Despite Cecily's warning, and my awareness, I was becoming addicted to the laughter, the personal attention, the good times I was having with Tillie. She never asked me to pay her way after the first dinner at Finn's when I had insisted on paying. She always paid her portion in cash, I noticed. That seemed unusual for a woman who traveled so much.

CHAPTER 9

Sometimes I wrote about Tillie when I was emailing Aida. She knew all about Tillie from my stories. I also told her about Cecily and about Dr. Geary and my work at Providence Hospital. I told stories about residents in the Memory Care and Rehab units. I told her about my efforts to enable people with dementia by teaching the staff to have them set the table for dinner, fold laundry and plant flowers in raised flower beds in our yard.

By now I knew all about Aida's everyday life too, about the narcissus she planted in Blue Ridge and about the rock slide she caused on the hillside of a customer's back yard.

One day in Aida's email she said,

- - - - - - - - - -

From <aidasadat@icloud.com

To <aubreygentile@hotmail.com

Aubrey, I really want to meet you. How do you feel about that? Can we do it soon?

- - - - - - - - - -

From <aubreygentile@hotmail.com

To <aidasadat@icloud.com

Aida, I'd love to meet you too but we're so far apart. I can't take vacation time yet. I have to earn it first. My job is so new.

Aida didn't give up easily. She wasn't forward about staying with me. Although it felt like we already knew each other quite well, neither of us was suggesting intimacy at this time. First things first and for us, sharing a bed was not first.

From <aidasadat@icloud.com

To <*aubreygentile@hotmail.com*

I can come there. How about early June? That should give me time to arrange my own vacation time and rent a hotel room. I don't mind if you have to work while I'm there. I'll sunbathe or shop.

"Tell her to come." Cecily was excited. "She's welcome to stay here if she wants. And you, my friend, can give her your room. You can always sleep on the couch if that's more comfortable for you."

"Right. And you said, I should choose girls for online dating who live far away so I wouldn't have to worry about dates. There's no way I'm inviting Aida to stay with us. This would be a first meeting. I don't want there to be any confusion about my intentions or mixed signals between us."

"Okay, arrange for her to stay at the Gilbert Inn Bed and Breakfast on Beach Drive. That speaks of class and it's historical. I bet Aida's a history buff. That place has four-poster beds, a tea room and a breakfast nook. The old house has been there as long as there have been whales in the ocean. Get her to stay at least a week so we can make a list of things for her to see and do, especially if you have to work any days I can keep her busy. Oh, Aubrey, she's going to love you, don't have any doubt about it." Cecily also had no doubt.

So it was arranged. Aida would arrive on June tenth and stay at the Gilbert Inn for a week. I walked around work with anticipation and elation. Aida was always on my mind. Cecily helped me make the list of things for her to see from the ancient, like The Tillamook Lighthouse built in 1890 to the modern, like The Buddha Kat Bar built last year. The day before Aida's arrival we filled the refrigerator with cheese and sausage for snacks, Lipton's green tea, white wine and Sam Adams, Salmon and fresh Pacific Perch and Rockfish and Cecily's specialty, pork roast. That was on June ninth, at Noon. Romance was in the air. On June ninth at two P.M. my phone rang.

"**Aubrey, this is Aida**. I'm so sorry to call you this late, but I will not be able to come this week. I have to take care of my sister's baby. There's no one else I can ask. I want to pay whatever you have to for the hotel if its past the cancellation date."

"Aida, you can't do this. We're so ready for you. We've bought lots of food that will go to waste. Your hotel reservation is all set up. We've planned for all of the tourist destinations and both Cecily and I have taken time off of work. Can you bring your niece with you?" I asked.

"No, it would be too scary for her. She doesn't know me yet. I'm afraid right now making a trip with me would be too traumatic for her. I'm sorry."

This was not just the end of a vacation but of the relationship for me, I was thinking. I couldn't say what I was thinking though so I just said, "I'm sorry too, Aida. Maybe we'll do it some other time. I'm sure you wouldn't disappoint me if you didn't have to. I have to go now, but please let me know more about this later." I quickly hung up the phone feeling devastated and didn't want this conversation to go on. I was too angry and trying not to express it. What kind of a justification was this? If she puts babysitting ahead of a month of my plans and maybe even the meeting of a husband-to-be? How could she do this? So much for staying detached from acquaintances just because they are online instead of face-to-face. I had felt like Aida might be my future. Now she was my no-way-Jose'.

Cecily read disaster on my face when she returned home from the office that evening. "What happened Aubrey? You look like your dog was inside the straw house that burned down."

I told her.

"How could she do this? Babysitting? Did she ever mention a sister before, or a niece? A niece that's that important to her? Is this just the best excuse she could dream up?"

Then Cecily went to her room to change into jeans. When she came back she said, "Let me pour you some wine."

We sat on the patio in Romeo's yard thinking, then Cecily said, "You know Aubrey, she should have let you know sooner, but I'm thinking, maybe she was afraid. You know being too vulnerable with someone you've met only online is scary. I was reading about the classic picture of a romance scam artist. It is often someone who works outside the United States. The scammer avoids meeting in person. They look for a person who does charity work because that's often a vulnerable person. The scam artist grooms the relationship for months and gets more and more intimate, might even discuss marriage. Then suddenly they come up with some kind of crisis and suggest that they can meet you soon if you help them with money to solve their crisis. The two of you are a combination of all of those characteristics put together."

"That sounds more like she's the scam artist than that I'm one. She should be able to trust me by now, Cecily. Heck, I haven't asked her for money and I haven't had a crisis."

"Aubrey," Cecily cautioned, "just wait it out a bit. You don't really know anything about this situation with her sister's baby and you were too upset to ask her. See if she asks for money, but don't offer her any.

"See if she tries to resolve this or offer you a better explanation. Don't lose contact yet, please don't Aubrey. She sounded so perfect for you. I'm so sorry this is happening."

"So much for your great idea of online romance," I chided Cecily.

"Well Aubrey, What can I say? I started all of this didn't I?" Cecily got up and walked around with her fingers to her mouth, thinking. "Do you want dinner? Under the circumstances we can have pork roast, salmon, fresh ocean perch almost anything you want…or we can hit the Brew n' Burger. But we have lots of food to eat up."

"Lets go to the Naked Wine Bar for starters, then we can come home and have cheese and sausage and crackers while we watch the waves. I better call Gilbert's Inn to cancel our reservation for Aida before we go out. I am going to let her pay for the room if they charge me."

Well that's what we did. But guess who we saw come into the Naked Bar. We were standing at a high table with six or eight other people laughing about some guy's vacation experiences with an outhouse when Tillie came ambling in. She didn't see us in the dim lighting but found an empty spot in a corner, sat down at a table by herself and ordered, what looked like a beer and whiskey shot. It couldn't have been more than fifteen minutes when she called April, the waitress over for a second and then a third. I had never seen

Tillie over indulge so I was surprised to see her like this alone, but then, I really didn't know her at all. Cecily discouraged me from interrupting Tillie to have her join us.

"Just watch her. Maybe this is why she likes to be with you," Cecily surmised. "Maybe she drinks too much when she's lonely but can control it if she's having a good time with other people."

We were about to leave. Cecily went out to wait on the sidewalk while I paid the check for us both. I noticed what I thought was Tillie's cigarette case on the table where she had been sitting. I was hoping to see her outside to tell her about it, but when I stepped outside Cecily and Tillie were standing on the sidewalk among other customers, talking with each other and my intention completely slipped my mind.

"We're just hanging with the 'in folk', Tillie said.

"Tillie's leaving for Yosemite tomorrow," Cecily announced.

"Yeah, I'll be there awhile this time. Why don't you come down and join me for a couple of days, Aubrey? Cecily says you have a few days off next week, it would be the perfect chance."

I forgot about the cigarette case. "Gee, let me think about it," I said hesitantly. *Can I stand three days with Miss Camoflage? Yet to be honest, I have enjoyed time with her here. It's just that I always feel like I have to explain her to other people. She looks so weird sometimes and she's boisterous. I wouldn't want to hurt her feelings though.* "I've never seen Yosemite. Maybe you could show me around. Where would I stay?" I finished the thought.

"You can make a reservation anyplace, then let me know so I can pick you up there and we'll drive into the park. No need for your car. Just hop the train, I'll have use of a car. Find a place near the Big Oak entrance because the motels at that entrance are closest to the Park. Hope to see you there." Tillie was off. She walked straight, didn't seem unsteady or drunk. I figured she could hold her liquor pretty well.

"I don't like it," Cecily said when we were heading home in my new red bug.

"Why? I'm not doing anything those days. And I'm certainly not waiting for anything to happen with Aida. Maybe it'll be good for me to let off a little steam for a few days."

"Aubrey, I don't like to see you get involved with that Tillie woman. She's not honest and she's hiding something. So, she makes you laugh. How about I just tickle you for a laugh? At least give yourself a few days to get in touch with Aida and find out what her full story is. Tillie in Yosemite seems to me like a rebound thing. Never a good idea."

After some thought that's what I did. This was Thursday. I would be off work next Wednesday, Thursday and Friday. That's when I would go to Yosemite. I could take a train like Tillie always did, stay at a motel for two nights and get a glimpse of Half Dome with Tillie at my side. Maybe I'd even fall in love if I got to know her better, contrary to what Cecily wants for me.

The next morning I hesitantly texted Aida:

"*I apologize for hanging up on you so quickly but I need more of an explanation than babysitting for you to cancel our plans. What's going on? If you want to call quits to our fledgling relationship please say so. If not, please say so. Just help me with more of an explanation.*"

Aida responded to me immediately by email:

- - - - - - - - - -

From <aidasadat@icloud.com
To <aubreygentile@hotmail.com

I could not make up the story of what has just happened to me. My sister Jocelyn who has been on street drugs for years, called me with 'her last dime' and asked me to pick up her daughter. I found her in a terrible place, an abandoned warehouse with junk all over the place and choking moldy and urine smells. There were about six other homeless people there all in as bad a shape as Jocelyn was. This little two-year-old was sitting by Jocelyn on the cement floor in a dress that was filthy, too large for her and no underwear. Her dark brown hair was matted, no shoes, long finger and toe nails, some bitten off. I had to step over used needles to get to the child and she screamed 'mama, mama,' when I picked her up to take her away from her mother. Jocelyn was so spacey that I couldn't manage her so I called 911 despite her protests, and they came with an ambulance to get Jocelyn. They let me carry the child and ride with them in the ambulance.

Jocelyn fought the ambulance drivers like a wild woman when they lifted her, but then collapsed completely unconscious in the ambulance. The emergency room was almost empty so they got to her right away, cleaned her up a little, started an I.V. All this time I'm walking around trying to calm down this dirty two-year-old. I must have been looking like a child abuser to anyone who was watching.

Jocelyn died in the emergency room. It was too late to reverse her drugs. She was dying of everything, so emaciated that she was having multi-organ failure. So now I have an approximately two-year old child. Jocelyn had no idea who the father is and she hasn't even named her, just called her 'the kid'. I don't know how this will turn out but I must take care of this child, probably adopt her if that is possible. She's my niece. I have to do this for Jocelyn. I've already been given temporary custody and a case worker.

I have enjoyed you so much online and looked forward to our visit this week. I can't ask you to get involved with me now. This situation is not something you bargained for when we started writing and I won't impose it on you. If you still want to write back and forth now that you know my situation I'd love it. My mom and aunt will be coming in town for a funeral next week so I will be taking care of them too. How did we ever get to this? My poor sister. Why couldn't she let me help her?

PS I'll have to name the baby. For now I'll call her Jahanara, which means to live or to flower. She looks kind of Middle Eastern, but nothing like Jocelyn. I could just call her Joy for short. Joy would honor her mom Jocelyn and a Mideastern name would honor her probable dad too and 'to flower' I hope, will be her. All three of them caught up in one name. And of course she'll have my last name, Sadat. I tried to ask my sister about my choice of names and she managed to mumble, "who, the kid? Yeah, whatever."

I'll send you a picture when I get Jahanara properly cleaned up, dressed, hair trimmed and a smile on her face, when she's flowering.

I'm going to love her but I've got a big job ahead of me to make this right for her.

I read Aida's email over and over. It didn't sound like a scam to me. I so much wanted to send her money to help out with the funeral and all, but I thought of Cecily's warning about the classic picture of scam romancers: seeking charity workers and saying they need money for their own crisis. On the other hand, if Aida was sincere, how cold it would be of me to ignore her now. I sent an email immediately just saying,

- - - - - - - - - -

From <aubreygentild@hotmail.com

To <aidasadat@icloud.com

I'm so sorry about your sister Aida. Of course we can write again. Just take care of yourself and your family and let me know how it all goes once things settle down.

Then I said for the first time: "*I love you.*"

I didn't know if I should have said it. I didn't want this to sound like a commitment yet, but she sounded so forlorn. It just came out of me so naturally, so uninhibited that it had to be the right thing to say even though I didn't know if it was true. For now, I had to get on with life, my life, while Aida was busy with hers.

What's a man to do? So many women, no woman. I would start planning my trip to Yosemite. I walked over to the local AAA office and picked up some brochures on Yosemite. I used the AAA office phone to make a reservation at the Traveler's Motel, as close as I could get to the Big Oak entrance suggested by Tillie. Travelers was the cheapest I could find, close to the entrance at $105.95 per night. Well, June near Yosemite, what could I expect? Besides I was only staying three nights. I would make the best of the tranquility and the vastness that was advertised. I would hike between ancient sequoia trees and not worry about the motel. Hiking in that terrain was probably enough to do for three days, without the need to plan for excursions that were advertised in the brochures, unless Tillie had other suggestions when I met up with her. I next made a reservation for a round trip in coach on the Starlight Express, leaving Seaside on Wednesday morning, returning Saturday.

The emotional trauma that this whole thing with Aida was putting me through made me restless. It was time for me to move out from Cecily's place and establish my own. I had a few days off now and wanted to keep busy so this was a great time to do it. I would find an apartment first, then maybe decide on buying a small place in town next year.

When I had gathered my brochures about Yosemite, I walked over to Cecily's Seaside Real Estate office to check out the listed apartments. Cecily was busy interviewing and touring a client, but the agent who interviewed me, Miles O'Brien was able to show me a furnished condo unit immediately available for rent. I paid the twenty-five dollars for my reference check but warned O'Brien that I had no U.S. work history or apartment history for the last eight years. I also begged him to wait until the next day to call for references from Providence and let me be the first to tell Cecily what I had in mind. I wanted to explain to them about my move, personally. Then I signed a one-year lease.

The Condo I leased was only ten years old and seemed solid, clean, bright and cheerful. It was inland, about a mile from the beach. That was good for me as a starter because the price was right, the closer you were to the beach the more you paid. My unit was on the second floor and had a wide-open view of the the blue, or sometimes stormy sky over the ocean from the living room. The snow on the top of Mt. Hood in the distance could be seen through the large bedroom window. The unit had hardwood bamboo floors throughout, white-walled bathrooms with all modern fixtures and the kitchen had matching Samsung stainless steel appliances. And best of all, I could afford it now that I had been working for a few months. I had a low interest loan on my Bug and had already paid for my computer and iphone. I also had a Visa. Boy did I need that Visa.

Cecily was happy for me to have found this rental. She didn't give me near the resistance about moving that I had expected. "All grown up with an apartment of your own," she said. "I feel like an empty-nester mom. Why don't you wait to move until you come back from Yosemite?"

I didn't want to wait. Now that I had a place of my own I was excited about my independence. The next day my lease was approved and I had time to waste until Wednesday before leaving for Yosemite. Cecily helped me move my computer and clothes on the weekend. We shopped together for new art supplies. The paints Cecily had saved from my dad's supply were hard and useless. I bought an easel, canvases and Arches 140 pound paper, brushes, oil, acrylic and water colors and a Sta-Wet palette. When returning from Yosemite I would have lots of scenic pictures to paint. I wanted to be all installed instead of having to think about a move when I returned from this trip.

I set my easel and roller cart up in the living room because of the ocean view through the sliding glass doors. Then Cecily and I met at my place for wine and song out on my shaded patio with snow-topped Mt. Hood smiling at us. We had brought the patio furniture home in her truck but the bed was delivered by Leaders. Cecily gave me a housewarming gift. It was a bankers box with four of everything in it, plates in two sizes, wine and water glasses, paper towels, flat ware, steak knives, towels and toilet paper rolls.

"Aubrey, you can always come back to my place if you need to," Cecily said. "It will be so great to have you in town wherever you hang your hat. A close friend to do stuff with, something I've never had here. Most of my friends in Seaside are clients who tend to be superficial and temporary."

I caught the train for Yosemite the next Wednesday. Cecily had offered me a ride to the station but I really wanted to start doing things for myself. I parked my Bug in long-term parking at the station and had Coffee and a sweet roll in the noisy, hot station café before train time. I was still feeling unsettled in life. This wasn't at all what I envisioned when I decided to leave Thailand. Yet, what had I envisioned? I felt jumbled, puzzled. I had a close friend, a great job for which I was well qualified, a smart apartment, enough money to get settled in a beautiful town that most people would give anything for and now I was starting out on an adventurous vacation.

Like I said before, I had three women and no woman. I sure didn't want them all. But the question hung in front of all that. Like a white king sized sheet hanging on a clothesline and blocking the view of the adjacent back yard, my future, so near, and yet it was hidden from me. What will you do with this wonderful life? What will you do with this gift of life?

CHAPTER 10

***A*fter having experienced the train rides in Thailand** with roosters under the seats crowing at sunrise and merchants selling barbequed sparrows through the windows at each stop, this train ride was uneventful but beautiful. The sun shone on the Pacific, as the water lapped on the shore and splashed on rocks. The sun behind the stretches of massive evergreen, silhouetted the trees. The earth to the right of the train where I sat appeared to be like streaked speckling because of the speed of the train. People in the train, children and grey-haired alike were awed and excited, jumping up and down from their seats or pacing the aisle. They were noisy, talked to and laughed with total strangers as if they were long lost buddies, comparing plans and previous experiences with the National Parks. This was the beginning of an adventure for them too. They could have put up with inconvenience easily but not with delay so it was fortunate that the train arrived exactly on time.

When the train pulled into the station and I deboarded it was three o'clock in the afternoon. I took an Uber ride to my motel, the Travelers. The motel looked like a cardboard box, plopped down on a gravel parking lot. The lack of landscaping belied its location at the foot of the purple and forested Sierras. I had to remind myself that I was paying a hundred and five dollars a night for the location near Yosemite, not for the view of the motel. At least it was clean, air conditioned and friendly, though the desk clerk did ask for full payment upfront. My room, like the outside of the motel was plain, paneled with dark fake wood, tan linoleum tile floors, a full-size bed that sunk a little in the middle and a clunky twenty-seven inch television set.

As soon as I had showered the train coach smell off of me I called Tillie. "I'm here and it's not dark out yet," I told her. "Can I meet you someplace?"

"I can't meet you now," she said. "Just relax tonight. How about tomorrow? I can meet you at ten A.M. Just check in with the motel clerk and she'll tell you how to get here. I have no wheels to get me to your motel. You can grab the shuttle bus that passes by all the motels on a schedule. When you get here in the morning we'll go hiking. There's a great trail that goes right by the Bridal Veil Falls. It's called The Falls Trail. Just meet me at the mouth of that trail. The shuttle driver can tell you where to get off. "

I hung up the phone without another word. Tillie's put-off was strange. What a relief it would be to have some time by myself. She didn't have to know that I'd rather have some time alone in this beautiful place. I had been wondering how I could make some time for myself without hurting her feelings. That night at the bar she sounded like she wanted the company so I figured I could put up with her for a couple of days. Yet her keeping her distance was not what I expected. There were always laughs when Tillie was around and maybe she'd be a great tour guide. What could she have to do that was more important than me? I thought she'd be more "with me" when I got here, excited to see me. I didn't know her, did I? Maybe her being a mystery woman was part of what both intrigued me and disturbed me, about her.

Anyway, I wouldn't have wanted to meet her here in this motel. No fun, no class. I'd rather spend whatever time we had together in the Park. Maybe Tillie had a room in one of the gorgeous upscale hotels in the Park that I had read about. Maybe this weekend would hold all kinds of surprises. I hoped they'd be good ones.

I decided to hop the shuttle into the park for dinner by myself. Maybe the Ahwahnee Hotel Dining Room would be too expensive for Tillie, or maybe just not her style. I'd go there while I was alone, splurge by myself tonight and forget Tillie. I made a six o'clock reservation for one in this amazing dining room. I figured I was worth spending money on, having a good time even if I didn't have a date.

The ceilings in this restaurant must have been at least thirty feet high. The tall windows that weren't covered with stained glass looked out on purple and red and orange rocks and mountain cliffs. They opened to the blue sky with shadowing white clouds. I ate with gusto, salmon caviar, then seared sea scallops with quinoa, an ancient rice, and asparagus. After dinner when I retired to the warmth of the common room by the huge stone fireplace I decided I was worth a dirty gin martini. My heart was filled by the music. I listened dreamily to the pianist's gentle rendition of Clair de Lune and then he burst out into "What a Wonderful World."

The ten o'clock shuttle delivered me back to cardboard box, which didn't feel so bad after all. Before I showered again, for the heck of it this time, I turned on the television and hit the brew button on the room's coffee pot. The tub was a little rusty but the shower water was wonderfully warm in this over-air-conditioned room. I sat on the bed pulled my legs up under the white cotton sheets and stuffed all four pillows behind my back. With dark Ghirardelli chocolate squares and coffee in a hand painted mug that that I had bought in the Park I felt totally refreshed and sleepy.

The news was on, always bad news. The police were looking for a killer, possibly a serial killer. A man's body had been found this morning in the wilderness at Yosemite National Park. Boy, that was too close for comfort to my temporary home. I changed the channel. I was here for a good time. I'd be with Tillie, I thought, when we went hiking. I'm sure she knows her way around and we'd be safe with so many tourists here at this time of the year. I checked out the weather channel. That was good news anyway. It would be seventy-eight degrees and sunny here the next two days. After being reassured on that account, I turned to a movie. Casa Blanca was showing on Public Television and I was asleep long before Bogart said, "I think this is the beginning of a beautiful friendship." I must use that line sometime, maybe even on Tillie.

CHAPTER 11

I **was awake by 6:30 A.M**. with too much time before I was to meet Tillie in the Park at ten. I walked over to a small restaurant that was down the road a piece. It was about the size of my motel and about as classy, but the bacon and eggs and grits were good. I brought a cup of black coffee back with me to the motel in my new mug then turned on the T.V. More news on that Yosemite dead body. Apparently, the reason the investigators thought the victim might be one of a serial killer's was that two other men had been killed in the same fashion, both by choking followed by back stabbings. Both of the others it was thought, were male prostitutes, one in the Sacramento area and one near Merced but both in rural areas. Well I have to admit the nearness to me in Yosemite had spooked me last night, but I could see now that this story really had nothing to do with this particular park, Yosemite. The other cases were far from here. I'd be careful and make a point of staying around other people, or at least with Tillie.

It was time to grab the shuttle and get to my meeting with Tillie at the Trail. Today would be fun. I put on my new hiking boots and wore jeans even though it was hot. Long pants for hiking had been recommended in the brochures. I wore a light weight sky blue Colombia shirt and had my sleeves rolled up and my old windbreaker tied around my waist just in case. I hopped onto the bus and explained to the driver where I was headed. The bus was full of excited adventurous people and soft-pedaled happy conversation.

When we arrived at the base of the trail the driver let me off in the midst of a large tour group. I searched through all of the crowds for Tillie but couldn't find her. I phoned her thinking that I might be in the wrong place but no response. I sat down on a chair-sized hard bumpy brown rock to wait. She must have gotten hung up someplace. After waiting an hour and making many phone calls to her I decided to check out the tour services at the hotel. I called Cecily on a whim while I was cooling my heels. "Why waste my whole day waiting for Tillie. There's a tour train that leaves from the hotel soon. I think I'll hop on," I told her.

"To be honest, I'm relieved," she sighed. "I was concerned about you and Tillie on a weekend at such a romantic spot. I don't like that woman and I hate to see you get too involved with her. She'll drop you the minute you're not convenient for her."

I didn't enjoy doing this alone as much as I thought I would. How long can you smile without your face hurting? And how many times can you say 'Wow'? How many other excited tourists can you tolerate when you're all alone? And how long can you meditate on trees whose lowest branches require a back bend to be seen? I spent the entire day doing all of the above. That was Thursday. I had one more day because my train left here Saturday morning.. If I talked to Tillie I would agree again to meet her but be prepared to find a way to enjoy myself alone. I couldn't count on her. So I booked a bus tour starting at the hotel at noon. She was obviously not excited about seeing me. I guess I had misread her intentions.

That evening after I got back to my motel, I repeated my routine of the night before. I was looking for another good movie to fall asleep to when the phone rang. Of course, it was Tillie. I didn't wait for her to speak. "A little belated, I would say, Tillie," "What happened this morning? Where were you? I waited an hour for you."

"Oh, I'm so sorry, Aubrey," she apologized, sounding very sincere. "I just couldn't get away from these people I was showing around. And anyway, the trail was so crowded with tourists it wouldn't have been any fun."

So she had seen the trail and the tourists. Maybe she had even seen me looking for her and didn't let me see her. She was really strange. And she was avoiding me. "Tillie I'll give you one more chance to hike with me. Tomorrow's my last day."

"Okay. Promise," she said. "I'll be there tomorrow. Why don't you just ask the driver to drop you off by the entrance to the park. I know the park well enough. We'll find a trail that's not so busy, no other tourists to bug us. It'll be more fun than hiking with all the crowds around. How's nine?"

"Fine, nine o'clock at the Park entrance. I'm catching a tour bus at noon by the hotel so I only have two and a half hours to hike." I let her know I had my bases covered.

I dressed in my hiking gear again on Friday, still hoping to find Tillie. I knew I'd enjoy my time with her if she ever showed up but I didn't want to get my hopes up. I got off the bus just within the entrance gate. It was total wilderness in that area, huge Sequoias, lots of shiny green holly with red berries, thick pine needle flooring from years of shedding trees. It was again a warm sunny day without even a white cloud interrupting the blue. I didn't see Tillie. I was hesitant to let the bus leave without me because I couldn't be sure she'd show up. I'd be stuck there without wheels. And I wasn't forgetting the warning about a murder here in Yosemite a few days ago. By this time the driver and I knew each other's first names. His was Morgan. Morgan agreed to pick me up on his return if I was still standing there, said he'd be looking for me and he'd see to it that I made it to the Noon-time tour I had scheduled.

Tillie showed up about ten minutes after I got off of the bus. Despite my misgivings I felt relieved seeing her. I didn't want to be alone in the wilderness. She was in an old blue Chevy sedan, scratched, dented, the side and back windows so scratched up and dirty that backing up in it would take a leap of faith for any driver.

"Hop in," she called. "I've got a great place in mind."

I opened the passenger door and got in, shoving mugs, papers, junk over to one side to make room for my feet. The back seats were full of stuff too. She couldn't have been using this car to show tourists around the park yesterday. Tillie was back in her camouflage gear, black tee, high top laced shoes, black socks. She had a huge canvas purse squashed between her hip and her left car door. About ten minutes into the park she turned right onto a small steep muddy path. She drove off road, as far as the car could weave and stopped, stuck, hopelessly stuck. She heaved her body back and forth in the seat, as if her weight could loosen the tires from the mud but her pitch and buck only dug us in deeper. We weren't going anyplace in this thing. I was hoping she didn't figure I could push the car. It almost seemed like she had deliberately taken us to a dead end.

Tillie jumped out of the car. It was stopped behind a clump of holly. I couldn't see around it to where she was going without getting out. "Stay right there," she said as I opened my door. "I need to check it out up ahead and see if we're in the right place. Besides, I have to do a lady's thing you know." She grabbed her big black purse from between her hip and the left car door and jumped out slamming the door. After walking about fifty feet she turned around and called back to me, "Just stay right there."

I was baffled. Why the caution? What's the big deal if I do follow her? Suddenly it hit me. It was her second precaution that struck me as odd. Without that I would have just waited for her to get back, been annoyed, maybe, but waited. I looked around the car, at all that junk in the back seat. She had a change of clothes, identical stuff to what she was wearing: a bra, a black tee shirt, black socks, camouflage shorts, brown high top hiking shoes. Everything she would need to change clothes if she got muddy, or bloody. What caught my eye especially was a pair of rubber gloves…and a shovel…and then I noticed a tarp, folded all neatly like it had just come from a store. And this car. Where did she suddenly get a car when she didn't have one to pick me up with earlier, or yesterday? And why not meet me at the park hotel, or at my motel, or on that busy trail? And what was so heavy in her big bag? It was not "a lady's thing".

    She returned to the car before I could get my wits about me. I had become nervous about hiking with Tillie. Who was she, really?

    "Okay, lets go, this is the place," she hollered.

    I cautiously stepped out of the car. What else could I do? I didn't want to follow her but then my curiosity and my fear got all jumbled up. I followed her. My brain would not work fast enough to come up with a plan. I carefully watched for "bread crumbs", for marks on trees, for anything that might help me find my way back if I decided to break away from her. I couldn't think quickly enough to come up with an excuse for not going at all. I was even afraid to let her see that I was afraid.

"Did ya ever make love in the woods? Tillie asked. "It's the greatest. I found a bare spot over here and put a blanket down for us."

"Tillie, I'm really not up to that right now. I'd really like to hike. Too many mosquitos to strip down in these woods," I pleaded.

"Aw, come on. We can hike too, There's time," she said.

I shook my head adamantly.

"Is it me? she asked. "How come all this time we never got around to making love and now here we are, the perfect time and place and you're afraid of a few mosquitos?"

I slowly slipped back away from her, not keeping pace, trying to lengthen the distance between us so that I would have a lead if I broke away.

"Keep going," I yelled, "I got a stone in my shoe. I'll just take it out and catch up to you." That didn't work very well because she stopped, walked back to get me, linked her arm through mine and pulled me along.

Sure enough, a few yards further and there it was, an army colored wool blanket spread out on the lumpy ground. It wasn't really a clearing, just a space big enough for a blanket for two where no sunlight showed through except a little mottling. Her big black bag was holding down one corner and rocks held down the other three.

"Just sit here and relax. I have a traveler's carafe of Merlot if you like.

I couldn't respond.

"We don't have to have sex if you don't want to, but maybe after a little wine you'll want to."

I sat uneasily on the edge of her blanket but I turned down the wine and pulled away when she tried to unbutton my shirt. She grabbed her black bag and pulled it to her side. Then she knelt behind me and started to knead the tight muscles of my shoulders. "I'll just help you relax," she said again, more soothingly.

What was in that bag that she just had to keep it hugged to her side?

I tried desperately to keep my voice steady. "Tillie, before anything else, I have to 'do a man's thing' if you know what I mean," I said to her.

"No you don't," she said, pushing me forward so that I fell sprawled face down on the blanket. As she fooled around with her fist down in that purse, she sat down heavily on my left ankle. I tried to pull my leg loose but she pulled a rope from her bag and looped it around my ankle. Before I could get loose, she wrapped the rope around a stake and pushed it down into the muddy ground. "Just some fun and games with my sex," she said, looking at my foot.

This was creepy. I was trying to remember what I learned in a self-defense class I had taken. '*Surprise is your friend. Move fast when its not expected.*' I laid quiet, long enough to let her think I was complying, then suddenly yanked my foot, bent my knee and knelt up all in one motion and with all of my adrenaline-saturated muscle strength I pulled the stake loose from the ground. Because the ground was muddy and soft, it worked. I was loose but was dragging that rope behind me. Tillie tried to grab the rope but it slipped from her hand and tripped me. My mind was racing through possibilities. I grabbed its end and moved fast twisting my body upwards. I was imbalanced but was able to grab onto a tree and head in the direction from which we had come. I hoped that I could find my way back in the direction of the car on the muddy road and then to the main road .

It couldn't be that Tillie was a killer, but she was. How do I run faster than she can track me or chase me with the car if its not really stuck? I turned and slid down the slight hill behind me. I had to get that rope off my ankle before it tripped me up. I had to get out of her sight. She would see movement but hiding quietly wasn't an option yet. The ground was slippery with wet pine needles. My heart was beating so loud, probably louder than a gun shot would have been. I was frantic to get out of her sight. Every stick I stepped on cracked like thunder. There was lots of holly. It was tearing my arms to shreds but I ignored it. If I was right, my blood on the holly might help someone find me. I could hear my own breathing. I bet she could hear it too. I was stunned to think that I, a tall and lithe enough man, could be running from this woman in fear, but it was fear. I was terrified!

I tried to remember the description of the murder victim. 'Male body found in Yosemite woods' the news line read. Did it say black male? Did it say serial killer? Did it say woman, knife, gun, shovel, buried, dragged, age forty…? Did it say anything I could liken to Tillie and me? Was I in a panic for nothing? If she realized what I had surmised, she would have to stop me and no doubt she had the means if she caught up to me.

Tillie was the serial killer and I was the living witness. Yes, she would have to stop me. I had associated with her, laughed with her and if I was lucky, I would be witnessing against her, but did I really have enough evidence? I slipped in the mud. In this dark, wild woods the sun cannot dry up the sludge between rains and my shoes were getting heavy with mud. I tried to stay on pine needles instead of mud but they were slippery and she was more experienced at navigating these woods. I had to make it back to the main road before Tillie caught up to me. She was close now, surely she heard me fall as I cracked a branch with my arm.

"Hey Aubrey, where you going? I thought you wanted to hike. Come on back. Help me get the car out of the mud and I'll drive you to the road if you changed your mind."

I was passing by her car. I hesitated there long enough to get the rope off my ankle. It was caked in blood from being yanked but I was able to slip it off. I trudged on. I had made it to the muddy path, now finally to the Park's paved road. There were no people in sight as I had been hoping. The run was downhill now, easier for both of us. I didn't know if she had a gun. If she did she would have a definite advantage now out on the road. Then I heard the first shot. It sounded like an explosion, the bullet roared so close to my ear, but it missed its mark. Now besides speed I needed cover. The instructor had taught me, '*Make sure you're never exposed. If she can't see you she can't hit you.*' I ducked into the line of trees along the road side but was slowed down to a weaving speed again. The brush here was almost impenetrable.

She called again, "Are you going to leave me here with my car stuck in the mud even after I drove all the way here just for you?" Hopefully she had lost sight of me and thought I'd answer her call to define my location.

I kept running and didn't answer, afraid even to hesitate long enough to extract my phone from a buttoned back pocket and call 911. Emergency Services wouldn't be able to get to me on time out here in the woods. How could I explain my location to them anyway?

She shot again, and missed again. Maybe she was a bad aim. Or maybe it was just that her pleasure was in the bloody stabbing, not in the killing per se, and she was still hoping for the prize, me.

Our distance from each other kept changing from a hundred feet to barely fifty, both of us choosing to wind through the woods now, rather than being exposed on the road. I was unnerved by her disappearance every now and then. I would think she was gone. I would slow down, and then she would emerge from the woods even closer than before and shoot again. Eventually luck would be with her aim, if not skill.

    The strength I had built up walking and biking those hot dusty roads in Thailand stood me in good stead now but Tillie was strong too. About a hundred feet from my drop off point on the main road into Yosemite, I took the chance, broke from the thicket and sprinted toward the bus stop. At the same point the sounds of gunshot stopped and Tillie disappeared into the woods again, not to return. As I ran back over the distance, this morning's ten minute bus drive felt like ten hours. With Morgan's free park bus no where in sight, afraid to wait out in the open, I slowed down to a walk and headed toward my motel but every step was with trepidation. Tillie knew where my room was. She knew I had a round trip ticket on the Starlight Express. She knew to where I would be heading. I had to disappear better than that until I could put some distance between us and think more clearly.

    Sweating, breathless and maybe crazy eyed I grabbed a local bus that just happened to come along the road. I felt certain I would be remembered by the driver and all the other passengers for my desperate appearance, sweaty, stinky, blood caked on my ankle and scratched up arms. If they were ever questioned by the police they would know they had seen me. The bus driver asked "Are you okay?" and I just nodded and walked to the back of the bus. I rode the local bus right past the motel to the Greyhound station in

Merced. From there I called the motel and explained that I would not be back. I told the clerk that they could just destroy the belongings I left in the room. I also cautioned him that no one was to be given any information about my departure or any personal information. I'm sure the clerk thought I was in big trouble with the police and being a black man, he probably figured I was guilty.

After purchasing a bus ticket for Seaside it occurred to me that I had a responsibility to make a police report as soon as possible. Who would believe me? A young lady that I had dated being a serial killer? But I had to tell someone before she found another victim. Trouble is, I didn't have any evidence. The only thing I had that could help with the search for the killer of the three men was her appearance and the location of the car. As much as I wanted to get away from here I had to do it, I had to speak up. I took a cab from the Greyhound Station to the nearest Merced police station.

I was interviewed there by a Captain Schoen who seemed very interested in my story. He sat me at a computer and asked me to write down a description of Tillie including her last name which I did not even know, and the events of the last few days. I wondered if he really intended to act on my story since he did not ask me to stay in town or speak to his boss about it. He probably wondered how I could have dated a woman and know so little about her. I gave Captain Schoen my correct email address so that I could be found by the police department if necessary, but I gave him a fake home address and phone number. I could not afford to have the police knocking on the door of my new apartment or calling me at work. I did not want anyone to ruin Cecily's life. Captain Schoen ushered me into a back room with bars on the windows and pulled out an ink blotter. He insisted on finger printing me.

"Why? I asked. I'm making a report on someone else, not on me. I'm the witness here."

"Just doing a little research here," he said. He walked across the room to a sink with a water faucet. Filled a plastic cup with water. "You seem nervous. Here, drink some water and calm down."

Next thing you know I'll be in a jail cell if I comply, I thought. Then how do I get out of this?

"Just wait right here and relax while I call my assistant to help you with those finger prints," he said calmly.

"Am I being arrested?" I asked.

"No, not unless we find something. Just a matter of security, then you can go," he said. He seemed to be trying to be casual.

I've got to get out of this now, I knew. I had asked the cabbie to wait for me. Hopefully he was waiting. When Schoen was out of sight I walked as quickly as I could while trying to look casual and headed to the front door. The cabbie wasn't where I had left him. I looked down the street and there he was. He had turned the cab around and was parked, headed in the direction from where we had come. I made it to the cab and jumped in. "Back to the bus station," I said as calmly as I could.

Cecily. I had to tell her right away, but I also had to get out of here, get far from Tillie as soon as possible.

I headed back to Greyhound. I had decided to take the first bus that was leaving for anywhere, just to get out of here, but guess where the first bus was headed. Seaside, Oregon. Before jumping on it I called Cecily at her office. She was in a panic. She had received a call from Tillie who was wondering if I had come back. Tillie told Cecily that she was supposed to meet me in Yosemite that morning and that I never showed up. Cecily then called my motel to speak with me, to be sure I was okay. She was told by the clerk that I was gone and had left all my belongings in the room and said they should be destroyed.

"I notified the Merced Police Department because I remembered the serial killer news item in the area where you were staying," she said.

"Cecily, I'm okay but I think that Tillie might be the killer." I described in a nut shell, the events of the last three days.

"Are you sure? Tillie? That can't be!" Cecily was flabbergasted. "But what if it is? Get out of there fast. I'll be at the train station waiting for you. I knew there was something wrong with that woman. She's a sociopath, that's what she is."

"I left my car at the train station so don't pick me up. I'm coming back on the bus. I'll go to the station to get the car and call you as soon as I get home," I said.

After a pause, to reassure Cecily I continued, "I made out a police report and notified my motel, then beat it out of town. I didn't give the police my correct address or phone number nor that of Providence, and I didn't give them any information about you. I wanted to be able to notify you and my job first, before you heard it from the police. I'm taking a bus back. I don't want to use my train ticket because that's the first place Tillie will look for me. Besides, the ticket is in my motel room and I didn't want to waste time going back there. Cecily, I'm so worried about you. Please feel free to stay in my apartment if you want. Tillie doesn't have that address and neither do the police."

"Romeo will take care of me and my house, Aubrey. Nothing will happen to me here. I'd rather stay in my house, but thanks for the offer."

CHAPTER 12

The bus ride back to Seaside seemed eternal as I could not focus on the beauty of the environment, only plan, worry, plan. I was sweaty. My brain and whole body felt like I did when I worked the night shift and had too much coffee and no sleep, but I hadn't had any coffee since breakfast and I had plenty of sleep the last two nights. When I arrived at my condo building ready to collapse the sky was already dark. I was looking at the moon like it was the last time I'd be free to see it. I fumbled with my keys, opened the door and there, bursting upon me, was Romeo jumping up and down for his long lost friend. I found out I could still laugh when Romeo put his paws up on my shoulders and started licking my face, his tail whipping wildly at the air. Cecily and Romeo waiting for me. What a relief. I dropped my luggage and sunk down into the nearest chair where I got a big kiss on the cheek from Cecily.

"I've been so worried," she said.

The Merced police called me, a Captain Schoen. He said he got this number from a woman who made a police report by phone. The woman said that she was reporting by phone because she was too afraid to stay in the Merced area or return there for an interview.

She described the man she was reporting as black, handsome, about five, eleven, narrow lanky build, dressed in hiking gear, and said he had abandoned his blue Chevy near a muddy path that led into the woods near the West entrance of Yosemite. She was afraid of him because he took her into the woods and wouldn't let her go. She broke away and ran. The police asked me if that fit the description of the man I know of as Aubrey Gentile."

"I didn't answer that question," Cecily assured me. "I just said that I didn't know where you were. I wanted to buy time to warn you before saying anything else."

"Fortunately, I made a police report too, mine was probably first," I said. "That should help them to see that I'm not somebody who is trying to run."

"I'm sure you were first. Captain Schoen remembered you. But I'm not so sure that will help when they consider that you lied about your personal information like phone numbers, employer and contacts.

"Captain Schoen told Tillie, I'm sure it must have been Tillie, to make out a report in person at the Police Department nearest to her present location. She hasn't done so yet. I just called back a few minutes ago and Shoen checked his computer for me. I lied to him and said I hadn't heard from you yet."

"Now, who do you think the police will believe? I'm a black man with no work history or location in the last eight years.

They will find my finger prints all over that abandoned car. I left my belongings in the motel and fled. I gave the police fake contact information for myself, my friend and my job. And then on top of everything else, I left the police station without giving my finger prints or DNA sample on the water glass as Shoen wanted me to. Their second report is from a white woman who is too afraid to come back to the area because the man in question, me, "wouldn't let her go".

"I don't want to involve you Cecily. You've gone through enough for me."

"Aubrey, you need me," she said. "You have only me to testify to your character and history. Without me you are suspect number one in at least three murders. Please let me help you with this. I love you too much to let this go down that way. Aubrey it won't, it can't. We'll figure it out together.

"Hey my life has been boring," she pinched my cheek. "At least until you arrived. No more boring now."

Cecily and I talked a long time, until two A.M. We never even got around to the beauty of Yosemite or my romantic dinner for one. My having a "number one status" as a suspect was too important. She and Romeo stayed in my place the night. Despite my total exhaustion and the fear going round and round in my whole tensed body, I fell asleep after about an hour. Cecily woke me at seven so that we could get on with our plan as soon as possible. I awoke wondering, how I would end this day, in my lovely apartment with my best friend and her dog or in a jail cell?

As soon as she arrived at work I met with the director of personnel at Providence. Dr. Geary was not yet available but I told his secretary Andrew that I needed an appointment with him as soon as possible and that it was very urgent. In case the police called before I could meet with Dr. Geary I left the information with the personnel director. I told her that if the police should call, she should give them any information they requested about my work. She should state that I was not in but could be found at the Seaside Police Station.

Cecily and I met at the station at eight fifteen. The station did not look like one that could deal with crime. It was pink stucco with a Spanish tile roof and yellow, white and purple pansies in gardens and along the winding path to the front door. When we stepped in the front lobby it was obvious that this had at one time been a private home. It was still decorated like one with comfortable couches and chairs scattered around the front room. It was the long tan plastic counter along the back wall with a half dozen computers and noisy printers clicking away that were totally out of place.

The first officer to the left looked up. "Can I help you?"

"I'd like to make a police report."

"I'll see if someone's available," she said disinterestedly.

"This is important like murder important, not just a lost purse." Cecily said insistently. She couldn't stand there and wait for the nonchalant small town attitude at a time like this.

After her outburst, we were quickly ushered into the office of Sergeant O'Leary. O'Leary had salt and pepper hair and thick mustache, a stocky man, not fat. He was red faced and dark eyed, dressed in uniform, cap and all. As we entered his office he quickly pulled his feet off his desk and hung up the phone without a word to the person on the other end.

"Murder? He asked.

We had carefully planned our approach in order to get O'Leary to take us seriously from the start. I began by telling him that our information had to do with the person that was being sought for murder in Yosemite and that I had just come from there.

"Why didn't you go to the police station there?" he asked.

"I did, but I need to add to what I told them. I had been too uptight to remember everything that is important," I said.

Now Cecily broke in with a little of my story She said, "You can trust him, O'Leary." Then she filled him in about where I had lived the last eight years, that I had been living with her and that I am now the Director of the Memory Care Unit and Rehab Center at Providence.

"Okay, so what's that all got to do with the murder in Yosemite?"

Then I told him about Tillie and our five month relationship and how I got stuck in the woods with her, how I ran from her, caught a bus, went to the Merced Police Station.

"So why would the Merced police call, Miss James here instead of calling you if they had more questions?"

"I gave them false phone numbers for my employer and my new apartment so that I could be the first to explain to my boss," I said. "I did give Captain Schoen my correct email address so that he could find me if he wanted to. I'm here now to correct the information I provided before."

O'Leary didn't want me to leave, at first. So that he could confirm everything I was telling him, we waited for him to call Merced. Then I begged my way out of the office, saying that I had an appointment with Dr. Geary. He called Dr. Geary to confirm that I truly did have an appointment and that he would be able to find me when he needed to. I could tell by the way he looked up and down over the half-glass frames of the glasses he wore, that he wasn't very confident that he was doing the right thing. I understood how he felt. What if I turned out to be the killer and he had let me slip through his net?

As we were leaving, I pleaded, "Most important, Sergeant O'Leary, please be sure that you all don't quit looking and trying to identify the right person. She's dangerous."

"Well obviously someone is dangerous. You and Dr. Geary will hear from us," O'Leary said.

When Cecily and I hit the sun drenched sidewalk and headed to her car I was so relieved that I had not been detained that my voice was quivering. "It was only because of his trust in you and Dr. Geary that I am a free man right now, Cecily. They'll never believe me over Tillie. She's a born liar. She'd pass every lie detector test."

"Yes, but she hasn't even been found yet. The police can't jump to conclusions based on a phone call from her."

Cecily dropped me off at the hospital and said she would wait in the café until I knew if I'd be working that day.

Dr. Geary was in his office when I arrived, dressed in a lime green golf shirt and grey pants. His strawberry blond hair looked more boyish with its short cut and cowlick when he was dressed casually. Today was his day off but Andrew had called him and told him that my message said a meeting was urgent. He had stopped in on the way to the golf course.

"I know you don't say 'urgent' if it's not, and my secretary said you called this 'urgent' so out with it Aubrey, what's up?"

I blurted out everything in my minimalist way, starting with the Seaside visit to Captain O'Leary and going backwards. He was somewhat skeptical, as the police had been.

"Aubrey, I sincerely hope as I'm sure you do, that this whole thing resolves without incident to you. You have to understand though, that if the police start showing up here, interviewing our clients or their families, disturbing you at work, I will have to ask you to take a leave of absence. It will disturb these family members terribly if they think I have hired someone who could endanger their loved one.

"Also, I will be in touch with the references you gave me in Thailand. I hired you based on your continuing nursing license without problem for eighteen years, your master's degree diploma, the character reference from Cecily James whom I have known and trusted for a long time and your own professional and knowledgeable self-presentation. It seemed too difficult and unnecessary to wait for your foreign references. It was a gamble I felt sure to win. However, now it's different. I may have to give an account for my decision to hire you if you are investigated. If I find anything askew I may have to ask you to leave. I would regret this deeply. You have been such an asset here," he said, and then continued,

"Our residents love you and the staff see you as fair and considerate. They say that you treat them as equals and take their ideas seriously. Just yesterday Ms. Stanford told me that she had an idea that was new here, to assign residents to specific staff who will take a special interest in them individually. She said you bought her idea, asked her how to set up the system and how to evaluate the system. She was so happy with her success and said that you were the first manager ever, to give staff people credit for their ideas and abilities."

After this mixed response from Dr. Geary I met Cecily in the café. My hand was shaking so hard I spilled some coffee but talking to her helped to get my feelings out in the open. I summarized Geary's comments for her and told her she could get on with her day. I would be here doing my job.

All during the day I watched the front door of the facility, expecting that at any moment I would see a couple of guys or gals in police uniforms at the door, asking for me. Apart from my nervousness, the day went smoothly, normally.

The next day I was called by Sergeant O'Leary and told to present myself immediately for fingerprinting. I managed to leave work without explaining my departure except to Andrew in Geary's office, and headed to the police department. I waited anxiously for an hour in the lobby of the station paging through several magazines that were there for the reading. I don't even know what magazines they were. I couldn't focus on anything but the suspicion this fingerprinting implied. The officer who fingerprinted me however, had no comments about whys or wherefores and acted like it was very routine. He did not detain me and I was able to return to work.

I spent three more nervous days, waiting to hear anything good or bad. I couldn't sleep. I spent most of the evenings with Cecily and Romeo. She invited me every day for dinner and playing with Romeo on the beach was a good distraction. Although I had wanted to keep her out of this, I knew, as she had said, that I needed her help and maybe her testimony.

Flowering

"You are not going to prison, Aubrey, Cecily said, then added,

"Have you told Aida about any of this?"

"God, no! Why would I tell Aida?" I asked. "She's not here. She doesn't have to know. It would scare her to death, to think that she almost came to visit a serial killer, and Cecily, I don't want to ruin my relationship with her. I'm starting to feel really good about her."

"I was just thinking that when this hits the papers it would help her to hear your side of the story first, she said."

"How will this hit the papers?" I asked.

Cecily just stared at me with that look that says, 'you dummy.' I should have known better. This would be big news in a town as small as Seaside. Who could keep the national media from picking it up? 'Local Man Being Questioned in the Murders of Three Men in California.'

"Aubrey, I know this is hard to believe and I know you're in shock, but you are also in big trouble. Please take it seriously," Cecily pleaded.

"Also, I have a lawyer friend that I am going to call for you. She's a real estate attorney so she won't be able to help you if this thing ever blows up into inditement. But she's smart and knowledgeable and she will support you and help you to know how to answer questions that are asked. Her name is Bea Smart. I'm not kidding, it's her real name. So if she calls you you should know that she is not some kind of jokester. It's her real name and she can help you, Aubrey."

Just when I was doing my best to not take it too seriously. Fortunately I took Cecily's advice about Aida. I emailed Aida that night. After asking about Jahanara, I told her that my trip to Yosemite had become a nightmare and that it was too difficult to explain the whole long scenario in an email. I asked permission to call her and explain in person on the phone. I told her that if she didn't hear from me she could contact Cecily and I gave her Cecily's contact information. I promised that she could always find out how things were going from Cecily.

Aida called me about midnight. I kept the story as short as possible but assured her of my innocence. I told her of my concern that Tillie might be a killer and needed to be caught before I could have any peace. I also told Aida how much I was coming to love her. Our relationship had been only from a distance but it was so important to me. I had to say it. She had to know it. And she said, "Me Too."

But, regardless of that I did not want her involved in this problem. I would not visit her or allow her to visit until all suspicion of me was laid to rest. Aida's life would not be complicated by mine.

When I hung up the phone it rang a second time. What did Aida forget to say? I grabbed the phone quickly so its ringing would not waken my neighbor and was shocked to hear Tillie's voice.

"Aubrey, I can sooo land you in jail. You just might want to let the police know that you want to, um, change the description of me that you've given them. And you know, change your story a bit. And by the way, I'd have that girlfriend of yours watch her dog."

My mind was racing. Do I speak to her? Do I threaten her? I remained silent for a good half minute waiting for more, while she waited, then she laughed and slammed the receiver. I tried to have the operator trace the call but he said he was unable. Said the call was coming from some untraceable phone.

Of course I had to phone Cecily right away.

"I'll take him to work with me," she said, resolving the problem quickly. I agreed that for now I would watch Romeo whenever she could not take him to work.

"Oh Cecily, I'm so sorry. We can't let anything happen to Romeo. Tillie must be in town. She knows how to find Romeo."

"Aubrey, he's a Doberman. She wouldn't dare hurt him. He'd maul her to death in an instant if she were to attack you or me or him."

"Don't trust her Cecily. You remember my fierce German Shepherd, Thor. My house was robbed with him sitting there in the kitchen. The thief must have given him a bone to chew or something. You can't count on what a dog will do."

Day five was D Day. Of course, I had been having a terrible time trying to sleep. I went to bed at eight, dozed off and awoke. I looked at my watch, surely it was about three A.M. Nope, it was eleven P.M. I tried again and finally really fell asleep about two A.M. Then I was awoken, startled at five in the morning by a clash of thunder. It was still pitch dark out but the fog was heavy and made the world on the other side of my windows look smoky. The wind was howling and blowing sand against my window, sounding almost like hail. I suddenly realized that there was pounding on my door. Maybe it was not thunder that had awoken me. I pulled on a robe and peeked through the vertical blind. There was someone at the door I had been seen looking out. "Police, open now." I opened the door partway first with the chain in place. When I saw it was really the police I opened the chain and they stepped in, dripping all over my bamboo floor and ready to cuff me. They agreed to follow me into the bedroom and watch me dress first before taking me in to the police station.

There I was, navy shorts, white tee shirt, running shoes, old windbreaker, hands behind my back in cuffs with rain pouring down on me. My arm was being twisted by the cop on the left who held onto the applied cuffs as he walked down the steps behind me. Right-side cop opened the back car door and shoved my head down to push me into the car, further twisting my arm. I could not sit back on the seat because of my restraints and I dared not complain of my position.

When we arrived at the station I was pulled by Left-side cop back to a bare-walled pink room with a man-sized cage at one end. Left-side cop grabbed my elbow, released one cuff and placed that hand up on a counter, all without a word. He rolled each finger over the ink pad and pressed it onto the form that said 'right hand' then cuffed it again. Then he did the same with the other hand. He cuffed me again and walked me over to the cage, shoved me in and removed the cuffs. Then he was joined by Right-side cop for the pat down. Believe me it wasn't gentle. I was stripped and sneered at for the search. When they were finished they let me stand there naked and walked out silently. I pulled my clothes back on. I was not offered coffee or food of any kind and I was not offered a phone call.

I felt like a side of beef being thrown into the meat freezer to await a customer who would take the cheap cut.

Of course, a local reporter was at Cecily's door by seven a.m. Cecily said she knew nothing and she didn't. I didn't have a chance to call her after I was arrested. She left immediately for the police station in Seaside where I was being held, taking Romeo with her. The police didn't want to let her bring Romeo in with her but one of the officers came to the doorway in front of the building so that she could explain the presence of the dog. The dog's life had been threatened making it necessary for her to keep it with her at all times. The officer agreed to put a guard on the car for fifteen minutes while she came in to provide her name and contact information as a witness for Aubrey. She also told them that Aubrey had a lawyer who would need to be called before he could be interviewed any further and provided her attorney's information.

Cecily repeated to me that she had an attorney that she trusted. "Trouble is," she said, "she's a real estate attorney, not a criminal defender. But she has agreed to interview you and represent you if you need someone at this stage of the proceedings. That way you'll at least have someone with you to protect you from answering questions that are meant to trick you. She will be looking for a colleague who is in criminal law to represent you before this case develops too far."

"My attorney's name was Bea Smart. Ms Smart came in about ten o'clock and visited me in my cage. She advised me to have a recorder placed on each of our land lines, mine at home and Cecily's, and not to answer the phones but to let the recorder give us the message. This of course, would not work on Cecily's business line because it would cause her to lose business. My incarceration and use of Cecily's generosity just could not go on for long without destroying both of us. I hated even hearing the term, criminal attorney. How did I suddenly become a criminal? I couldn't believe I had been booked in a murder investigation.

It seemed that the Seaside police were being given orders by the Merced police. The only evidence that they claimed to have against me was my finger prints which matched those that they found in the abandoned car. They were also suspicious that I had given them false contact information for myself and that I had left my motel so abruptly and so could not be contacted that way. Also the phone call from a possible witness against me was of concern. Suspicious behavior, they called it.

I now was on leave of absence from Providence Hospital. I would soon lose my apartment and car if I was unable to make payments. Cecily was being glared at by neighbors and felt that there was a drop in her business, though she could not say if it was related to our connection.

The Seaside Weekly had a headline the next day, which read: PERSON OF INTEREST above my picture on the front page. It did not say arrested. What did they call my predicament if not an "arrest"? Any perceptive person could read between the lines of the article and see that the police had no substantial evidence against me. There was no body but there could be evidence of assault in the location of my fingerprints in the car. I don't know what Tillie left in that car. Surely she cleaned her own prints off of it. If there was evidence of assault from Tillie's previous encounters in the car, could the investigators tie that to me? No evidence of ownership could be found in the car, serial numbers all having been filed off and none of Tillie's prints were found.

At the conclusion of each of my interviews and there were many, I begged everyone to keep looking for Tillie. Police were unable to identify her in their data base and the name Tillie was not of much help without even a last name. According to the media the usual suspect in this case was either, a peddler, a female homeless person or a homosexual person. The victims had been choked and stabbed but not robbed.. The police were not suspecting a wife, a thief, or, I don't know, a gypsy, a savage, a park employee. Where did I fit in all this?

After forty-eight hours I was released on bond, paid by whom? Of course, Cecily. Though all evidence was circumstantial, I was warned not to leave town. Of course where could I go? I still had my apartment and car. Much as I hated to accept her money, Cecily insisted that she keep up my car payments and rent.

Aida kept writing. She had seen my name in an item about the murders of the three men whose bodies were found in California. However, the item she read had indicated that I was a person of interest for the possible information that I might provide rather than as a suspect. The fingerprints found at the scene of the Merced murder had not yet been identified but were not a match to mine according to this article.

Aida wrote to me.

- - - - - - - - - -

From <aidasadat@icloud.com

To <aubreygentile@hotmail.com

Aubrey, I want so much to visit you. I hope it's not in a jail cell but I know that just can't be. I will come wherever you are. I told Jahanara about you and she wants to visit you too. You can't believe what a beautiful child she is now that I can see her skin without all the dirt on her. She has huge brown eyes and I'm braiding her dark brown hair in a French braid just like mine. I think she is learning to trust me. That is coming slowly. She had no idea what a refrigerator or microwave oven were. She probably never had hot or cold food. She has gained four pounds. She had never slept in a real bed or been in a bathtub. I am now her official guardian or foster mother. DNA testing has been done on me, on Jocelyn and on Jahanara and confirmed that we are related so I don't think there will be any problem with adopting her unless a father shows up. The search for him is going nowhere.

Here she is talking about how slowly the child is learning to trust her. How can she believe in trust like she does? How can she trust me without ever even having met me? It frightens me to think how easily Aida could trust the wrong person. As much as I wanted to keep in Aida's good graces, I didn't like that she was so willing to trust a man she really didn't know.

- - - - - - - - - -

From <*aubreygentile@hotmail.com*
To <aidasadat@icloud.com
Aida, how can I ever thank you for your courage and for caring enough to keep up with me. This long distance relationship of ours has not been easy. You have never even met me and you trust that I am good and innocent. I hope I can make it up to you someday. I worry about you though.

Please be careful. Don't let everyone into your heart as you have done with me. Sometime it could be the wrong person.

From <aidasadat@icloud.com>
To <aubreygentile@hotmail.com>
Who are you, my mother?

You kept writing to me too after you had reason to doubt my sincerity. Maybe we're both rescue freaks. I admit I had someone check into your history a little when I first heard about this. I never doubted you but I was advised that it was common sense since I now have a daughter. So you can rest on that account. I know it is all going to be okay.

CHAPTER 13

***It* was a week after my release from jail** that Cecily had an ap-pointment in Seattle with the Northwest Tourist Commission. She asked if I would stay at her house to take care of Romeo, walk him, feed him, clean up after him, buddy him. I was depressed, restless and anxious because of the turn my life had taken. Me, Mr. Gentile, Manager of the Memory Care and Rehabilitation Units of Providence Hospital, nurse to poor people with Malaria and Leprosy, the good guy, the one everybody could count on, admire, how did I become 'the wanted'?

I lay on the bed in Cecily's guest room and watched the sun flickering on the waves, sparkling on the sand, but I just felt like running. It was the first time I remembered wanting to just run away from everything, from life. I had too much pent up energy just lying here not being able to fix this. 'What will you do with this wonderful life?' Who first asked that question? I had to do something with this trauma. I had to learn from it. Even in jail my life would have to be meaningful. I owed it to my parents, to Cecily and Aida who had put so much trust in me.

My brain circled round and round giving me a headache, my eyes had trouble focusing as I turned back and forth on the bed. I was trying to come up with the reasons I should have hope, should be grateful. All the reasons just rolled into the big black hole in my spirit. A serial killer? That could only mean a death sentence.

Mentally I cocked the pistol that could end it all. I wouldn't go there, couldn't think about that. Not even possible. I turned toward the window. I would force myself to think of something else, like the pair of cardinals sitting on the picket fence.

Romeo had followed me into the bedroom and lay down on the floor beside the bed on the side that was away from the window. He was behind me. First he pawed my back. *C'mon pay attention to me.* Then I heard him put his paws up onto the bedside cabinet and knock something down. I heard the paper rattle as the something fell. "Oh, come on Buddy. Do you want to get on the bed?" I said to him. I turned over to see what damage he had done and saw, there on the floor, a white bag. I opened the bag to peek at its contents, to be sure nothing had broken. There inside was the small black shiny Chinese case that Tillie had used to carry cigarettes in. Romeo looked up at me with that begging expression, front feet leaping, tail wagging. *A new toy. Please throw it for me. I can fetch it for you.*

Suddenly I remembered, urgently I remembered! That night shortly before Yosemite, when Cecily and I had seen Tillie come into the Naked Wine Bar, when she probably had a little too much to drink, she forgot the cigarette case on her table when leaving the bar. As I paid the bill I saw the case that she had forgotten. *Oh, I must tell Tillie, that she forgot her case,* I thought. I walked out of the bar that night and found Tillie and Cecily talking together, I had forgotten to tell her about the case. She left without it. The next morning the bartender called Cecily. "I think your friend left her cigarette box on the table last night. Do you want to pick it up for her? I don't know how to contact her.

So Cecily had gone by the bar the next morning and retrieved Tillie's cigarette case that had been bagged for her to pick up. Cecily probably left it there in the guest room for me to return to Tillie and then forgot about it.

Finger Prints!

I wonder if Tillie could have left fingerprints on her case. I dare not touch it myself. I left the bagged item on the bedside table, took Romeo out of the room and closed the door. I gave Romeo my best guy hug. He hit me with his paw to tell me that the hug wasn't enough, he also wanted a treat for the good job he had done. I gave him a big hunk of roast beef from the refrigerator. Then I texted Cecily and left her the message.

Tillie's cigarette case is on the bedside table of your guest bedroom. I don't dare touch it and leave my prints so I closed the door and took Romeo to my apartment. If Tillie's prints are on the box, it might help support our story. The bartender could confirm the description of the person who left the box. He could corroborate the date and time that it had been left. He would be another witness to my story.

When Cecily returned, we called the Captain O'Leary and asked them to retrieve the box in whatever method they used for forensic evidence.

"Captain O'Leary, I may have some tangible evidence tying Tillie to me and to my story."

"Sure Aubrey. What would that be?" he asked.

Cecily got on the line. "O'Leary, please take this seriously. I want your forensic guy over here now. This is important."

O'Leary, captain or not, knew how to obey Cecily. The detective was sent right over, took our little white treasure in his plastic bag and said we would hear from him "soon."

It took another anxious three days. I wasn't eating, wasn't sleeping, wasn't thinking clearly. Seamus, (Dr. Geary) called to be supportive. He wanted me to come for lunch with him. Lunch? I'd vomit at his lovely lunch. I couldn't look him in the eyes. I'd see pity. He'd see guilt. Cecily couldn't help me anymore so she went to work and came home pretending everything was normal. I felt like my whole life boiled down to that one little cigarette case...

When the landline phone rang I didn't answer it. What if it was Tillie again? Maybe this was the time for my return to Thailand. Surely the search wouldn't find me there and bring me back just to answer charges with only circumstantial evidence. Tillie couldn't prove anything. With my heart racing, fibrillating, I sat down by the phone, looked at the phone and thought about the phone. What if Cecily was in trouble or needed me, or something happened to Romeo? I'd have to answer it if it rang again.

Flowering

CHAPTER 14

*T*hen **my cell phone rang.** It was O'Leary. He was so hesitant, clearing his throat stumbling on his words. I knew it, no fingerprints. Next thing he would tell me I was to be picked up and not to leave town. Then he got the words out: "Well Gentile, you can relax, we got fingerprints from the box," he grumbled. "There were two sets of prints. One of them belonged to your bartender friend. We've already checked him out. He's okay."

Another pause. *Com'on out with it O'Leary.*

"The other fingerprints on the box you gave us?" Pause. "They matched those found at the Merced murder scene. The prints belonged to someone by the name Margaret Wilber who was wanted in Utah for check forging. Miss Wilber has an extensive rap sheet but nothing bordering on murder. She would never have been a suspect in those three Calfornia murders without the fingerprints on that cigarette case of hers. We haven't found her yet to get a DNA sample. Nothing's certain until we have DNA but at least we have an idea where to look, who to look for. You done good for us Gentile. Never thought you had it in you. I figured you didn't murder anyone but sure didn't believe you knew who did. Hope you learn to pick your girlfriends better next time."

Did you ever hear a man cry? I mean really sob?

"What's the matter, Gentile? Thought you'd be glad, "he bellowed when he heard me.

O'Leary said that Margaret Wilber also had a juvenile record of cruelty. "Interesting story," he said. "When she was a kid she killed the little white rat that was a mascot in her fifth grade classroom. The children, her classmates, took turns caring for the rat and when it was her turn, she reached in, grabbed it and wrung its neck right in front of her classmates. She had to be transferred from that school because the sight of her and the memory of her cruelty disturbed the other children so much."

I kind of heard O'Leary but I wasn't quite sure how he had jumped from me being free to Tillie killing a rat in her childhood. It didn't matter. I hope I thanked him.

I flipped the phone closed and waited for Cecily to get here. She was coming over after work just to be with me. I couldn't even call her or Aida or Geary. My arms were too weak to pick up and hold steadily, even my cell phone. My voice was too shaky to speak in an unbroken sentence. I was like a new born babe, flailing around. I couldn't grasp the idea, a whole new life with possibility ahead of me. What would I do with this wonderful life?

I hung in the chair like a rag doll. Tomorrow I'd paint again. Tomorrow I'd call Aida. Tomorrow, yes there would be a tomorrow.

When Cecily walked in the door she must have thought I had been found guilty because my affect looked like a guilty guy. My energy had been so zapped during the last three weeks. While the threat of a life or death in prison ended suddenly with a few words, my rise from horror to a good life again would not be so easy. For all those weeks I had been falling deeper into despair while trying to tell myself I would rise again. When I told Cecily about O'Leary's call she cried too. She insisted that I come to her house to celebrate so that Romeo could be there with us. "After all, it's his fault that you're free, isn't it," she said.

The next day Cecily called Bea Smart to ask her how to get my booking off the records. She was concerned that my future could be clouded by a police record even though the end finding was "not guilty." Ms. Smart was given more information about Tillie during her conversations with Captain O'Leary. Tillie's adult crimes had to do with assault, stalking and abuse. She had spent nine months in prison after leaving a car parked on a train track causing injury to several people when one of the train cars derailed. She was caught that time when a horrified witness saw her get out of the car, watch for the train and laugh with her fingers in her ears as she heard the train screach to a halt, not soon enough, then plunge into the car.

The description given by the bartender as well as the pattern of Tillie's visits to the bar was placed in evidence to support my story. In addition, Dr. Geary had received a response from the church in Thailand and from the government hospital after his urgent request, which confirmed the date of my arrival and my continuous presence in their village.

Margaret Wilber was now wanted for questioning in the stabbing death of three men. She was too crafty to get caught murdering again anytime soon. I hoped she was clever enough to lay low forever. That would keep Cecily and Romeo and me safe. I would have been her number four victim, I was sure. Fear of a new relationship, fear of the unknown, had collected in my psyche, had stomped on me. I was her fourth victim even though I had escaped being murdered.

I was reinstated in my job. Dr. Geary raised the roof with the Seaside Weekly. "Since you put a picture of Aubrey on the front page with a title like 'PERSON OF INTEREST,' you better put a bigger one there now that he has been cleared. A third page item won't do. I want you to show what a hero he's been (his words, not mine, I would have called me a 'wimp') during this uncalled for misjudgment of him." Dr. Geary also wanted to insure the reputation of his hospital Memory Care and Rehab. Units of course.

The next morning on the front page of the Weekly my picture was printed again under the headline, INTERESTING PERSON. The body of the article indicated that Providence was proud to have as its Director of the Memory Care and Rehabilitation Units, a 'world renowned nurse' who has plans for making our facility totally inclusive. "It will be a comfortable home to professional people and manual laborers, rich and poor." According to Dr. Geary,

"All of Seaside will want to live here when he is done." The article also noted that I had provided information, which hopefully would lead to the arrest of Margaret Wilber. The picture of Tillie that they used for the article was taken from her booking in the train wreck incident. Pretty homely. She was of course, persona non grata in Seaside and was unlikely to show up here again.

Except for the need for constant vigilance with Romeo until Tillie/Miss Wilber was found, my life seemed to be returning to normal. I wasn't sure what normal was though. What else could happen?

CHAPTER 15

Aida's emails had been consistent and familiar during this entire episode even though I had not been very responsive. When I told her the whole story in detail starring Romeo, she said:

- - - - - - - - - -

From <aidasadat@icloud.com

To <aubreygentile@hotmail.com

I knew it, Aubrey. Please call tonight if you can. I want to hear your voice. I just knew, from all these months of sharing with you that you had to be innocent, had to be the man I think I've grown to love even from a long distance. Pour yourself a glass of wine before you call me and we'll toast to new life together.

Wait til you hear my latest baby story. I never had a child. This is so much fun. I've been wondering what I should have Jahanara call me. She still remembers Jocelyn as Mama and I'm not sure I want her to lose that memory. But maybe she'll lose it anyway and if she is to be my adopted child, I should be Mama to her. Also she's been asking me about Dada and I don't know what to tell her. She solved half of the problem for me. This morning she called me Mamada. I don't know how she came up with that. When I first took her home she asked who I was and I told her that for now I would be both Mama and Dada for her so she would have both until we found a daddy.

From <aubreygentile@hotmail.com
To <aidasadat@icloud.com

Dear Mamada, I will phone you about ten if that's okay. I love the 'babycoin'. Did you receive the pictures yet that I sent by snail mail? They're all recent. I sent pictures of my friend Cecily and of her house and mine so that Jahanara can get used to us before she comes to visit. I do hope we can make it possible soon. I'm so looking forward to your visit.

From <aidasadat@icloud.com
To <aubreygentile@hotmail.com

Three times Jahanara has asked me, "Is Oh Me my Dada?" I couldn't figure out what she meant. Maybe she did know her daddy and he said "Oh Me" a lot. Yesterday I received your pictures. I had them all spread out on the dining room table. Last night she climbed up on a chair and was studying the pictures. I stood behind her watching and she got all excited and pointed with her sticky fingers onto the picture of you and said, "Oh Me, Mamada. Oh Me." You must be Oh Me, as close as she can come to saying Aubrey.

She's heard me saying your name a lot. When I read your emails I tell her, 'This is a letter from Aubrey' or when I talk with my mom or a friend on the phone I tell them about you and she listens intently. So she has names for both of us now, Oh me and Mamada.

She wants a daddy so badly. The other kids in Day Care all have daddies.

From <aubreygentile@hotmail.com
To <aidasadat@icloud.com
Aida, your note almost made me cry.

From <audasadat@icloud.com
To<aubreygentile@hotmail.com
Aubrey, don't be too complimented by Jahanara's comment. Today she pulled a chair over to the refrigerator, climbed up on it and pointed to the picture of Romeo that I had put up there on a magnet and asked, "My Dada?"

Oh me, Oh my, I must find her a daddy.

From <aubreygentile@hotmail.com
To <aidasadat@icloud.com
Aida, I'm not sure how much time I can take off of work after my leave of absence but please plan to bring

Jahanara when you come. The two of you can enjoy Cecily's house on the beach when I'm at work.

- - - - - - - - - -

From <aidasadat@icloud.com

To <aubreygentile@hotmail.com

How's August first? Keep sending me lots of pictures of you, the house, the beach and town and Romeo and Cecily. That will help me get Jahanara ready for this first meeting.

"First meeting." Aida was obviously thinking there would be more. What would happen this time to prevent her visit? One couldn't do much worse than last time, a newly orphaned child, a possible murder and a stint in prison?

CHAPTER 16

P*reparing for Aida's visit* was easy this time, a re-run of the first attempt. We filled Cecily's refrigerator as we did before but this time added mac and cheese and milk since a child had been added to the brew. We also filled my refrigerator. We had two homes now. Aida and the baby would stay at the Gilbert Inn as previously planned. We would have most of our meals with Cecily both to include her, my closest family, in the visit, and to give Aida and Jahanara time to become comfortable with me in a family setting.

Every step of my preparation for this visit seemed to be of weighty consequence, like what should I wear when meeting Aida. Any other time I would have asked, *"What should I wear? So what."* But now it was, long pants or short? White or dark? Formal or casual? It was summer in a beach town. I wore navy shorts, a white short-sleeved cotton shirt, sandals. I arrived at the airport way too early and paced between arrival gates watching for each change in time, place and cancellations for all the planes, not just hers. I knew the plane from Chattanooga would be cancelled, but what if it arrived? What would I say to Aida first? I tried out everything, quietly but out loud: "Hi, you must be Aida." Or "Welcome to Portland." Or "I love you." No, that would ruin everything. Or...

Then the plane landed. I moved to the back of the fifty or so waiting friends and family to watch the deplaning, to watch each individual step out of the ramp luggage in hand, then grabbing and kissing their person. There must have been about two thousand before Aida stepped out, or at least twenty. When I saw her I plunged into the standing crowd and wiggled my way to the front, my feet tripping on each other and lagging way behind my head.

She was dressed like a female me, navy skort, white lacy cotton blouse, her black shiny hair in a French braid as on her pictures, olive skin both from her genes and from her daily work in the sunshine of Copperhill, Tennessee. She had a yellow and white frangipani blossom tucked into her hair above the left ear. She carried her two–year-old twin in her right arm and pulled a rolling suitcase with her left. The child in a yellow tee and jeans shorts had a finger in her mouth and bright eyes searching the crowd.

As Aida came closer to me, I saw all of my longing in her black eyes. When she saw me, the moisture welled up in them releasing one silent tear. Jahanara pointed at me and cried, "OhMe, Mamada, OhMe!" Aida dropped hold of the luggage, put Jahanara down at her side, took my hand, looked into my eyes and said just, "Aubrey." I said, "Aida," and somehow the world kept spinning. After an eternity, or at least a lifetime of looking into each other, I bent down to give Jahanara a kiss on the cheek and then did the same for Aida.

I took hold of the larger suitcase. Jahanara refused to be carried but she took my hand and pulled her own little suitcase. "The car is parked in the lot, come with me," I said to Aida. Those were my first words to Aida, *The car is parked in the lot, come with me.* After all my dreams of what I would say to her, all my practice, all my anticipation, all I could say was, *the car is parked in the lot.* Was this what love at first sight was meant to be like?

I am grateful for the conversation of little children. The hour and a half drive to Seaside was filled with whys and hows and what's thats and of course questions about Romeo. We drove first to the Gilbert Inn. Aida's room faced West, overlooking the beach and ocean but was full of sunshine even though, at only eleven o'clock in the morning, the sun was in the other direction..

I sat in the only chair in the room while they settled in. Aida placed Jahanara's things in the bottom drawer in the chest of drawers so that she could choose her own clothes in the mornings. Jahanara placed her little plaid flannel pajamas under her pillow on the side by the window, her own choice. She put a little rag doll dog on her pillow to guard the p.j.s. She carried her toothbrush to the bathroom. The bathroom became a feminine one very quickly. It smelled of lilacs. The whole place was remodeled and redecorated within a half hour. My role was to wait, to be amazed and silent. When they had settled in, job complete, Aida stood in front of me, made a big "wheew" and said, "okay, what's next?"

"May I kiss you?" I asked.

She didn't answer but reached for my hand and pulled me up from the chair. She put her arms around my waist, looked up at me and nodded. Our first kiss was warm, genuine and deep in our hearts. For several minutes we searched each other's eyes and were fully absorbed by each other's souls until our second kiss was like a gigantic, colossal 'yes'.

"Next is forever," I said.

When we arrived at Cecily's house she was already home from work and busy in the kitchen fixing shrimp and cocktail sauce hors d'oeurves for us. We were holding hands by the time we arrived at Cecily's house. I had barely introduced Aida to her when there, on Cecily's front doorstep, the three girls became lifelong best friends, right before my eyes. How amazing! We enjoyed our first visit out at the white wicker table in Romeo's yard. As we shared the details of the morning trip and plans for the week, Romeo lay lazily in the sand with Jahanara sitting at his side petting his long back and singing to him.

"I heard there has been a huge earthquake in Alaska," Cecily told us, an 8.2. That's almost as big as the 1964 quake. I don't know the details yet. It was on the news just before I left work. I didn't wait to listen to the details because I was hurrying to beat it out of there. I wanted to get home early to meet you, Aida and Jahanara."

"Good thing we're far away from it, Aida said. "I understand earthquakes can cause those tsunamis and tsunamis can be deadly for people who are in striking range. Those poor people in Alaska, and what happens to the bears and seals and other creatures? They must be so frightened," Aida mused. Cecily and I looked at each other with alarm in our eyes. The thought had startled us both at once. A tsunami? The 1964 quake in Alaska had caused a deadly tsunami all along the Canadian and northern US American coastline. But we didn't want to frighten our guests unnecessarily. Quakes don't always result in tsunamis.

"We'll keep the news on so we'll know if there are any more quakes or threats of tsunamis" Cecily said.

CHAPTER 17

While Cecily fixed dinner, the rest of us drove over to my condo and had all those getting acquainted conversations. Aida's grandparents had immigrated to the United States from Iran with their two baby daughters forty years ago, just before the revolution. When the Shah headed the country the women had been free not to wear the traditional hajib. Both her mother and Aunt Pari were nurses. They had discarded the practice when they started nursing. Although wearing it was allowed, these two ladies felt that it was kind of a nuisance at work, just like nursing caps that female American nurses wore at that time. Head covering was enforced again after Ayatollah Khomeini took power but by that time Aida's mom's family was in the United States. Both women passed their boards here with no delay and worked in American hospitals, Pari in Los Angeles and Aida's mom in Nashville. They became Americanized very quickly.

The next generation was Aida, her sister Jocelyn and her brother Emil. Emil who married a Persian woman and returned to Iran where all of his wife's family still lived. It was very sad for

Flowering

Aida, she said, that her brother and his family were so restricted now and so far away that they were unable to see each other. When Aunt Pari retired, she moved to Nashville to be near her sister. Both her mom and aunt are retired now and live in the Nashville area together since the death of Aida's dad.

At seven o'clock as requested by Cecily, we returned to her house for dinner. After dinner, we toured Seaside in her five seater Ram since Jahanara insisted that Romeo go with us and there was room for him in the Ram back seat. We promised Aida a walking tour of the trendy shops, the light house, Main Street and the promenade the next day. I took the girls up to their room at the hotel while Cecily waited outside in the truck with Romeo. I tucked the baby in bed, kissed Aida goodnight, pulling away from her with great difficulty. I wanted kiss number three to last forever. After all this time, a whole life of waiting for both of us, we both knew we had met our first mate. A few hours ago I had wondered if I would ever meet someone that I could love forever and build the rest of my life with. Now I knew without a doubt. We had forded every stream, followed every rainbow. We would have to wait at least one more day for the pot of gold but we had found our dream. There would be tomorrow and then another six days of learning all about each other. Then there would be forever.

When I arrived back downstairs to the truck, Cecily was out by the beach wading and watching the water. "Aubrey, this is not low tide," she said warily. "This is a weird wide beach created by a receding surge. Watch. When you went upstairs I took off my shoes and came out here to wade at the edge. While you were gone the water came all the way to my knees and now it's back out again even further. You weren't gone long enough for this much change in the water level to take place naturally. This isn't normal tide."

"There haven't been any tsunami warnings, have there?" I asked her.

"Not yet. I've been listening for them. If it happens the warnings will be loud and clear. Seaside is now equipped with good monitoring systems, the IPAW system and of course social media alert. We should be okay if we just keep in touch with the systems. We can't stop our lives on a dime every time Alaska or Japan or California have earthquakes."

We arrived back at Cecily's house about eleven. We got out of the car and walked out to the beach. The water was only a little higher than usual. There were no waves at all. There were no crashing sounds. The moon was full and light came from shore, from homes and hotels glaring on the black smooth Sea. It was way too calm. But there was a lot more trash up on the beach than usual including some large logs that had to have tumbled in from north of here. A water surge must have flooded this beach while we were gone."

"I'm really worried about Aida and the baby. Do you think I should take them up to my place for the night?" I asked Cecily.

"Aubrey, that will really frighten them, she reassured me. I'll set my alarm clock for two A.M. and check for warnings. We can both leave the television on while we sleep to catch any news if we awaken. Romeo can walk out here to the beach with me when I'm up at two. We'll have to awaken Aida during the night if there are signs of trouble but let's let them sleep awhile. It's been a big tiring day for them. Why don't you get some sleep too just in case. Tomorrow may be a long day."

"I don't know if I can sleep now I said. I've had lots of practice not sleeping."

"Sleep. If we're really getting into crisis mode, the town crier siren will be so loud you'll know it. So will Aida. I'm sure she'll call. If it is looking bad at two, you can wake her by phone and I'll get right over to the hotel and pick her up."

At almost one thirty I awoke and checked my phone. No service. I got up and checked the television. It was black. No service, no communication, no time. I threw on my jeans, boots, sweatshirt and rain jacket. I grabbed my car and house keys and my phone just in case I got a connection, and headed out to the Gilbert Inn. I needed to get to Cecily's too, to be sure she was awake but at least she had the truck. Aida and Jahanara had no means to escape unless an evacuation vehicle came by. If they boarded a rescue vehicle I might have trouble finding them afterwards. They were my first responsibility.

I was almost to their hotel when the siren blared. Dot dot dot dash dash dash dot dot dot cardiac arrest cardiac arrest cardiac arrest. My heart thumped as loud as the siren, at least I could hear it as well. I couldn't even call Aida. When I got to the hotel I found a bus in front loading the guests. There were two more buses behind the first waiting to load guests. The hotel staff were all outside waiting for the last ride. I jumped out of my bug and started searching among the waiting, panic. Then I heard the baby voice screaming, "Oh Me! Mamada." They were just about to step onto the bus. Aida was holding tightly to her purse and to Jahanara. Jahanara with arms around her mama's neck and looking over her shoulder, was holding her little stuffed dog. I rushed over and pulled them out of line and wrapped my arms around both of them together, but just for a second. I loaded them into my car. They had been instructed by the hotel loud speaker system to dress and come down to the lobby quickly and without luggage.

"We have to get Cecily, I told them. I have no way to call her. She planned to set her alarm for two o'clock but another half hour may be too late."

I drove inland first, expecting that road to be a little safer than the coastline road, then I drove north toward her house, where hopefully the traffic was not as bad. Even in that direction the traffic was stop and start all the way. The people were amazingly courteous, stopping for cross traffic and trying desperately to lay off their horns. I could feel the panic in the way the cars screeched when stopping and jerked when starting. I could feel the panic because of my own acute concentration and the stare of my frightened passengers burning into me.

When we got to Cecily's the house was lit up but the truck was gone. The water was up to her doorway, about forty feet from its normal shoreline. I jumped out and pounded on the door and windows just in case she was in there but no one answered and no dog barked. Good, she was gone, I hoped to my place. I turned and drove toward home. The drive inland was worse than the drive to Cecily's but, though the street was packed, the flow of traffic was in my direction. One mile an hour. Was a mile inland enough distance for us to be safe? I had to get Aida and the baby out of here. How? An hour and a half to the Portland airport? Would we ever get a plane ticket with all these people clamoring for a seat? We couldn't even call ahead to reserve one.

Finally, we arrived at my condo.

No blue Ram truck.

"Aida, I must get you out of here," I said, trying not to sound hysterical.

'I'm not leaving you, Aubrey," she said.

"No Mamada. I want Romeo. Find Romeo," Jahanara contributed.

"I hope my condo is far enough away to be safe. Why don't you wait here while I try to find Cecily," I said.

"We can't just leave town without her," Aida said.

I was about to open the door for Aida and Jahanara when I heard the most eerie sound I could have imagined. It was thundering, deafening like an approaching locomotive just about to hit you. A high pitched scream ran through it like a train's wheels screeching on the iron rails when the train brakes. It was devoid of all human and animal sound. All humans and animals must have been in shock because I didn't hear any of the screams or barks I would have expected. Then I saw a wall of water. It was just there, black, with moonlight making it look shiny like tar. One second I was looking downhill at a town of structures, shops and homes speckled with a few porch lights. The next second I was looking at a black wall, like the underside of a mountain ripped from the earth and laying on its side. I grabbed Aida and Jahanara and pulled them up behind my condo building. If the wave came this far maybe we might crash against the building instead of floating away with the wave. Then the locomotive sound turned into a crashing sound, then swoosh, swoosh, swoosh. We were soaked but we were still planted on the earth. We hadn't floated away. We hadn't drowned. We hadn't even fallen. And we hadn't found Cecily and her dog and truck.

We stood silently holding on to each other for a long time. Then Aida asked, "Is it over?"

"I think so," I said. Stay right here and hold onto this rail. Sometimes a tsunami comes in several waves. I'll walk around the building and have a look."

"What was left of the town still had lights. The electric plant was built further away from the sea than my building. You could see lights in a few houses to about two blocks closer to the sea than mine, then black, flattened land with moonlight shining innocently on the tragic landscape. The town was gone, all gone. One of the eerie things about this whole humongous happening was that there was no storm. It wasn't raining, it wasn't cold. We had pleasant hot summer weather. How could this happen? Why did the god's not send weather, like storms and thunder and lightening, to match our tragedy? And where were Cecily and Romeo?

Then I heard a car horn beeping from behind my building. I was worried about my ladies, wanted to be sure they wouldn't get into someone else's vehicle. I ran back to check on them and there was the blue truck with Romeo hanging out the passenger side toward us. I ran to the truck and hugged him, the sobs just burst out of me while Romeo lapped up all the salt and wetness from my face. "Where have you been?" I screamed angrily. I was angry at Cecily like one is at God after the death of a loved one. "I thought I lost you."

"Hop in," Cecily yelled to us. We're getting out of town now! I've plenty of gas and the truck will be much safer than that little thing you drive. One less car on the highway if we ride together." I put Aida and Jahanara in the front with Cecily.

"I'm going upstairs to grab some blankets, clothes, food. We don't know where we'll end up tonight; we might need them if we end up sleeping in the truck. I'll be down in a second."

We didn't know where we would drive, just east, just away.

CHAPTER 18

***I'm sure my house will be gone**, Cecily said."

"But you're not gone, its just a house, I said." I didn't mean to make light of her loss. I knew this was a trite thing to say. But what could I say that would help? This was devastating for her, her home and her place of business the life that she had sacrificed for and built up for years, ever since her hard earned college education.

"What now?" she asked

"Just head for the first motel we can find that has a room" I said.

We found one that "left the lights on for us" seventy miles and three hours later. We all checked into one room, first of all because there was only one available room. Besides that, we felt safer that way.

The shock of the trauma was still quieting us. We could hardly speak even to each other. The shock would be around for a long time. We probably, theoretically could have stayed at my place, it seemed safe. But we couldn't.

We all had this feeling like we had to get away, we had to move, we had to do something. Like the whole world could still collapse around us and on us if we stayed too close to it. We somehow had to be at some distance from it all, to look at it from the outside in order to figure out the reality of what had happened. In just a few hours we had become one, we had one history, one pain, one awe, one unimaginable experience that would stay with us for the rest of our lives.

We all slept together in one king sized bed, Cecily on the left, then Aida, then Jahanara, then me. Romeo of course, jumped up on top of our feet as he was used to doing. I mean we slept together, not as in sleeping together but as in togetherness. And we did sleep, until two in the afternoon. We would need to stay for another night. It was too late to drive back once we were away, had eaten and breathed.

The tsunami hitting Seaside added to the tsunami in my life. How could I bring this unsuspecting woman and her child into my series of tragedies? An undeveloped country may be the best place for me where people live day-by-day tragedies and know how to deal with them. They had a phrase in Thailand: *My pen ry*. It means it doesn't matter. Whatever happens to them they say '*My pen ry*'.

But here in the States? My parents killed in a car crash, my date turned serial killer, myself in jail, now when I think I may have found the love of my life, a tsunami. A TSUNAMI. If I had tried to write a book about a series of tragedies I could not have dreamed up this list.

The next day I said to Aida, "I think we should take you to the Seattle airport. There are still no seats available out of Portland. I'm so sorry this has happened to our dream. I think I'm a disaster in your life that you don't need. Maybe my life will settle down one day and we can try again if you want. But I want you to be free of me for now."

Aida looked totally shocked at my statement, shaking her head no during my entire blabbing discourse. Her eyes opened wide and she took a deep breath and punched me hard on the chest. "Do you think I would leave you at a time like this? What do you think I am? Do you take our love so lightly? I am not leaving now. I am going back with you to Seaside."

"But Aida, I will be needed at work more than ever now. I don't even know if Providence survived or if our residents are still alive. And Cecily's house is probably gone. If it's gone she'll need a place to stay and she'll have to stay with me. But most of all I'm thinking of you and the baby. You have a job back in Tennessee and Joy needs some stability in her short life. This thing may take a long time for me to resolve."

"Aubrey, Jahanara and I are going back to Seaside with you. The child can be the least of your worries. She is a pro at adjusting. This child thrives on new experiences and on caring for other people in difficult times. We'll take one day at a time we'll work out the problems as we find them, but we won't leave you now," Aida insisted.

"Cecily, see if you can talk Aida into leaving. You may need to crash in my place if your house is gone,"I said, trying to get Cecily's help with protecting Aida.

The ladies stuck together, Cecily presiding. "Aubrey, we can make room for all of us at your condo if necessary. We're pretty sure that it has survived. When disasters happen, townspeople help each other. Don't sell Seaside short. You'll see everyone turning out to help each other. I can find another place to stay if need be.

You can't send Aida away until she's ready. Don't do it on an impulse anyway. Let's just get back and see what's next. You and Aida may have just met each other at age thirty-six, but you've already filled in the gaps of the first thirty-five years. You've had enough experience together for anyone's lifetime."

CHAPTER 19

***W*hat would happen next,** and what could we do about it anyway? The first thing we did was drive to Cecily's house. It was gone, flattened. It was hard even to locate its exact previous location. It was just a big beach strewn with clothes and curtains that were blowing around and kitchen appliances and bathtubs. There was nothing much to pick through. The back of a tipped over refrigerator, the handles from a broom and mop sticking out of the sand. Most of the stuff probably wasn't even hers.

Cecily walked silently around, kicking up sand. It looked like she was searching for the perimeter of her house. She hung on to the top of the wrought iron fence that stuck up above the sand. She didn't say a word, couldn't.

"Cecily, we'll help you dig through this and see if we can find any of your things," Aida offered. She too was distressed. Neither Aida nor I could imagine what it felt like to see your house like this, or rather not see, your house at all like this.

"No, Aida," Cecily finally answered, "not now. It's too painful, too devastating to even think about. In my new life everything will have to be new anyway. I'd never get all the sand

and mud and muck and mold out of whatever is left. In time I'll think about coming over here to search. Not now."

That night Cecily stayed at my house with Aida, Jahanara and Romeo. Aida and Jahanara had my room, Cecily had the guest room and I had the couch. Romeo gave us turns having the privelege of his snuggly warmth. My computer was working and Cecily had to send out messages to her staff and clients to let them know that she could not answer questions just now. She promised that in a week she would give them information about the status of their jobs, vacations, housing or refunds. There was absolutely nothing she could do about her house except take pictures and speak by phone with insurance agents' recordings instructing her to "push one, push two" for information. Well that was frustrating when you've just lost your house and everything you owned.

Aida insisted on going with me to Providence to see if she could help in any way. She and I walked into town heading to the hospital but the proper word was not "walked". We climbed over things and trampled and shoved our way into town. Aida was wearing jeans and a grey sweat shirt and running shoes that she had had the presence of mind to wear when she dressed quickly the night of the evacuation. I too was in jeans and running shoes, the easier to climb over obstacles.

All of the ocean front shops were either completely gone or had been smashed or flooded right up to the ceiling and would have to be torn down. Logs and stumps and lumber and glass had been stripped away from homes and shops and were tossed everyplace making it impossible to drive into town. Furniture, pianos, upside down cars and trucks and buses were everywhere except where they had started out, like cars hanging out of windows, a bed on a roof top and a bathtub on the beach. Swimming pools had emptied, the water sucked out by the humongous wave as it returned to sea. The small bridge over a creek through the back of town was gone. The structures further from shore that were still standing had been inundated with sand and smelled of rotting dead fish. There were only three deaths reported at this time, three too many. Lots of people were reported missing and the search was on for bodies "door to door," but these doors weren't standing vertically. ...And the sun still shone.

Unbelievably, the historic Seaside Promenade had survived. It was covered with sand, several feet in some places, but had not caved in. This was the sign that the people of Seaside needed. Seaside would return, its history in the form of its Promenade and the Tillamook Lighthouse and the Lewis and Clark Memorial remained.

Providence Medical Center? It was now sitting on beach, no lawn or flowers, the sand having been washed up over the first three blocks of the town. The older part of the facility where my residents had been housed was smashed to smithereens. The Rehabilitation Unit for which I was also responsible had been evacuated and was not yet re-opened. When the new administrator and the board met to determine the future of this Medical Center, a decision would be made about the format their Rehabilitation Services would take in the future. Mrs. Dagoob said I would be needed in this decision making process but for now the unit would remain closed.

One of the three known deaths from the tsunami was Dr. Seamus Geary. He had stayed on duty to be sure every last patient in the hospital, every resident in the Memory Care Unit and every staff person was evacuated before he would leave. I had failed him, failed my staff and residents. I wasn't here when they needed me, I was tooting around town with my visitors showing off my pride of ownership of this town to which I had so recently arrived. How could I even show my face in the Hospital? The guy who wasn't here when we really needed him. When I had found Cecily on the beach that night after taking Aida and Jahanara to their room and sensed the danger, I should have come to work, should have thought of evacuating residents, should have

My grief for Seamus who had befriended me both on my arrival to this country and town and also through my arrest and incarceration would have to wait. There was so much work to be done. I had to keep going, had to do something to help, had to work, or I would crash. I felt like I was carrying on my back, all the people Dr. Geary would have helped the rest of his long life if he had been allowed to live. I should have been here.

Aida knew that look of devastation on my face. She knew I was holding back tears as I stood staring at the empty shambles of my residents' building. Windows were smashed, the welcoming red front door hung lopsided, bricks and aluminum strewn all over the place. She shouldn't have had to see me this way so early in our relationship. She should have had my smiles to remember, not my irresponsibility and shame.

In the absence of Dr. Geary and the part of the structure where I had worked, I searched for the current or interim Administrator who turned out to be Mercedes Dagoob, the previous manager of finance. She seemed happy to see us, showed no signs of blame but gave both Aida and I a job to do. The main hospital record room was intact and contained all the files from the residents in the Memory Care Unit. Aida used her cell phone which was working again and began canvassing the contacts that had been listed for our residents, to determine their safety and what we needed to do further to assist them with housing. I took an assignment in the emergency room which had been overflowing since the tsunami. During the first twelve hours the patients were mostly victims of near drowning. There were parents, spouses, friends, grandchildren looking for lost ones. Later it would be people with injuries from falling objects, large cuts from rusty gutters and nails and carport roofs and still, people searching for lost loved ones.

On this first day back to work after the tsunami, we were exhausted by the time it was dark. We headed back to my apartment, climbing over mountains of trash between the hospital and my home, promising to return the next day. The next day Cecily insisted on taking Aida's place so that Aida could stay with Jahanara. Cecily said this child was truly a flowering joy like her name said and she'd like to have about ten kids just like Jahanara. This child had spent her day sitting by the dog, offering him treats and telling him that everything would be okay.

The entire week progressed in the same way, Aida and Cecily alternating days to help at the hospital. I went everyday and was able to put my nursing skills to good use again. Each day I came home too exhausted to eat dinner, stinking with sweat and people's blood and grime. Each day I heard more crying than I had in all of my life before that time.

By the third day the streets had been cleared enough that we were able to drive to the hospital so that we were a little less tired arriving home. Now it was time to attempt again, this conversation with Aida. Although our love for each other was growing powerfully, this was not an atmosphere for romance. It was hard to imagine when we could allow romance to happen.

"Aida, don't you think it's time for you to return home?" I asked her.

"Aubrey, why don't you come with me she offered."

"I think I am still needed here, Aida."

"When will you not be needed here?" she asked.

"I'll know when the time comes," I answered.

"Aubrey, I think you're working yourself to death thinking that somehow you can make up for the loss of Dr. Geary. You are

Flowering

not at fault, Aubrey. He was that kind of a man, a man who would eventually have given his life for someone else if not for the people of Providence Hospital. It would have happened whether or not you were here. If you were here he would have insisted you leave and then you'd be feeling guilty for leaving. Maybe if you get away from here for a while you can grieve properly for him instead of trying to make up for his loss with your overwork.

"You're avoiding the truth and blaming yourself. Maybe you're still blaming yourself for Jaum that boy you told me about, and for all the people you left in Thailand. Maybe you're blaming yourself for the Tsunami, for God's sake."

I wouldn't allow the truth of what she said to sink in, to ease me.

"Aida, isn't a tsunami enough punishment for you? Do you still think you need to give me another chance? Can't you see that I would be a disaster in your life?" I asked her.

Aida thought awhile, trying to find a way to reach me. "A tsunami is part of our universe's expansion, a part of our evolution. We and our world are all empowered to care for each other. That's what makes us more good, more like God. We can only enjoy and be responsible for our little corner, not everyone else's corners. Eternal Love will take care of the rest. Aubrey, trust your experience of love, trust Dr. Geary's decision to give himself, trust us, you and me, trust us."

I wasn't ready to listen.

"Aida, I still need to be here. Cecily needs to be here and I want to help her. The hospital staff is still stretched too thin and I am feeling really needed, more than I ever have since I left Thailand."

"Okay Aubrey, Jahanara and I will leave," she finally agreed. I have wanted so badly for us to have the rest of our lives together but maybe you're telling me that you think this isn't meant to be or that it is not important enough for you to make it work."

Aida hadn't given up on me yet. "Please come to see me in Copperhill as soon as you can. I want to give us another chance. I love you so much. But I can see that this work you're doing makes you feel fulfilled. I don't know if I can compete with that, Aubrey." *And I wonder if I'm competing with Cecily, she was thinking.*

And so I took Aida and her Jahanara to the airport in Portland. It was a difficult trip for all three of us. We hugged goodbye and only glanced quickly into each others eyes. My chest was heaving and my muscles were taut with the attempt to be nonchalant and hide my emotion. Would this be a goodbye forever hug? Only Jahanara could express the way we all felt. She just cried. That said more than the words couldn't say.

CHAPTER 20

Three months had passed and Seaside was making amazing progress in repairing itself and its life. Some tourists had booked time for the holidays and even for next summer. Cecily and Romeo were still living in my guest room. She had found an office to rent for her business and was hoping to buy the building as it had been vacated by its previous owner. She would then be able to make a temporary suite for herself and Romeo. It did have a view of the ocean, although it was not right on the beach as her dream house had been. Being a Seaside life timer, Cecily would never leave here because she loved so much about it, the seasons, the summer sunshine and beach. The people who lived here year round were friendly but not intrusive. I had a hunch she also felt that she would have a better chance of being found by her son Bobby if she stayed in one place.

Emails between Aida and I continued almost daily but were usually somewhat superficial and sometimes philosophical, not laced with the longing that I still had and presumed that she did too. Without the amor, it did not seem to be like it used to be.

- - - - - - - - - -

From <aidasadat@icloud.com

To<aubreygentile@hotmail.com

Copperhill is coming to life again. I thought it would never grow back to its "glory days" with copper mining gone. But we now have a new restaurant on the Ocoee River with a walking trail over a bridge for waiting diners. And we have a couple of new trendy shops in town in the midst of all the antique shops. Those older places are filled with just used tools and rakes and tractors. Success brings success though. If the new places do well, there may be more. I'm hoping. Jahanara misses you and Romeo. She asks about you all the time, wants to come and visit again.

From <aubreygentile@hotmail.com

To <aidasadat@icloud.com

Aida, Maybe its my turn to come there. I'm ready, but I don't want to impose and don't want to bring any new disasters into your life.

From <aidasadat@icloud.com

To <aubreygentile@hotmail.com

Aubrey, nothing you do or bring to me could ever be considered a disaster in my life. Don't be a victim of the sadness you feel for other people. The suffering ones we will always have with us, but they shouldn't overshadow our lives. We have been given so much joy and should be respectful of it and grateful for it. We should live our lives joyfully.

Cecily too, was urging me to visit Aida in Tennessee. I kept planning and then postponing the trip. We often sat on my balcony for a first cup of coffee in the morning before heading to our jobs. Cecily's agencies were both housed now in the old building she was planning to buy. She had an overwhelming amount of negotiating with insurance companies and clients to do. Cecily was unbelievably creative. As a real estate agent she was able to convert a contract for a destroyed cottage on the beach into a vacation in Paris. As a travel agent she was able to convince people with a contract for a former beachfront summer home, that what they really wanted was a cruise on the Rhine River.

I was still working in the emergency room of Providence. This was not what I had been hired for, but at least I could be useful here. It was not my favorite place. I found it stressful. The staff was very short handed. As time would tell, the staff who remained in town were never ending in their generosity, working every shift needed but many of the staff had had to leave town with their families, their homes gone. All of our previous Memory Care residents had either been placed in another facility or their family members had decided to keep them in the family home. The new administrator of Providence had not yet figured out if the building of a new Memory Care Unit would be financially warranted. He was not a Dr. Geary. The bottom line was his primary concern. A new hospital addition to house these specialties would be expensive.

"Maybe I really belong in an underdeveloped country," I said to Cecily one morning. "I just can't get excited by all this vacation stuff and I'm not an emergency room kind of guy."

Cecily must have wondered about this before. "Aubrey," she said, "why do you think that in eight years in Thailand you never painted? You took almost no pictures. And when I asked you about it, you said that there wasn't much beauty to paint or photograph. That isn't like you. The real artist Aubrey would have been enthralled with the things you were living among every day. Children climbing in a garbage pit looking for food, women building a church, families sitting on the ground with a bowl of rice waiting for a clinic to open, religious brothers and village men digging a well together, silk weaving, buffalo. You are a real artist, how could you not paint? Don't tell me it was because you were busy nursing. I know you. You're an artist.

She continued, "First thing you wanted to do when we set up your new apartment was to get some art supplies and get started painting. And what attracted you to Aida so strongly? She is beautiful, inside and out. That baby of hers should have her portrait painted. Those big brown eyes full of sincerity, those puffy pink cheeks and one dimple that make her smile a little crooked. And when she's excited, how she stretches both arms to the sky. Paint her Aubrey."

"I didn't have the energy to paint when my days ended in Muang Iai, I said."

"You didn't have the psychic energy or the emotional energy. The real artist in you would have found more energy with a paint brush in hand not less. It would have relaxed you to paint. No, you felt isolated. Although you loved the place and the people, I think you were lonely. I think your desire to ease all the pain in the world trumped your ability to stand up for yourself, to respect your own needs and desires.

You didn't give yourself credit for your own skills and your need for joy.

I think you should paint again, Aubrey. Get out there in Seaside and find a place that still looks devastated. Find the beauty in the survival out there and paint it. Or paint the beach and the ocean. When you get excited again by the beauty you can see and can create like no one else can, it will be easier to know who you really are, what you really want. I think you're too melancholy. Going back over there to the Orient would be the easy answer. You need a challenge to become your old refreshing self again.

"And what about Aida? she continued. Are you just trying her out?"

Cecily wasn't mincing words. She wanted to force me to think about this, to do something about it. Was I being fair to Aida?

Was I just filling an empty space with her? Why really did I come back from Thailand? Did my loneliness trump my self-respect like Cecily said? What would I do with the rest of my life if I loved myself as much as I loved the poor? If I loved myself as much as my parents loved me? As much as I think both Cecily and Aida love me?

"I can't just run off to Tennessee at the instant I think of it. I have to work …and I help take care of Romeo," I said, tongue in cheek.

"Hog wash!" she said.

"Go and visit the love of your life, Aubrey. She'll know what to do, how to help you," she added.

That whole day at work I was distracted by that conversation. I arranged to take two days off work, the first two I had taken in three months. If I was really gloomy it was not the time to visit Aida. I better do something about it. Cecily was wise.

I wrote to Aida:

- - - - - - - - - -

From <aubreygentile@hotmail.com

To <aidasadat@icloud.com

Aida I'm starting to paint again. Cecily wants me to paint a portrait of Jahanara. Maybe I should arrange a trip to visit you soon? Can you put up with me for a whole week so I can get that started?

She answered:

From <aidasadat@icloud.com

To <aubreygentile@hotmail.com

A week? How about a year? I know you can get a nursing job here if you want to. The home care agency of Maryville is always looking for nurses who live in rural areas more distant from the Medical Center. And don't sell Copperhill short on opportunities for artists either. After dusk almost everyday in summer, one can see all the plein air artists from Murphy, North Carolina hanging out around town and on the side of the mountain. They paint the river's edge and the homes on the mountainside.

From <aubreygentile@hotmail.com

To <aidasdat@icloud.com

I'll do it. I'll come, but I'm only going to plan a week for now. How about October twentieth? Is that a good time for me to paint the red and orange and golden- leaved trees of Copperhill?

From <aidasadat@icloud.com

To <aubreygentile@hotmail.com

Perfect. I need to establish a birthday date for Jahanara. We have no birth information. Jocelyn apparently delivered the baby right in that empty warehouse with the help of the other addicts. I can't believe that baby survived. The doctor said the best he can tell she is about three years old now so I'm going to make up a birthday date for her and have it put on a birth certificate as soon as the adoption is final. What if I make the birthday date October twentieth and you can surprise her. Your visit will be her birthday present.

From <aubreygentile@hotmail.com
To <aidasadat@icloud.com

I'm so excited.

Excited, yes, and I was scared. "So excited" didn't begin to say what I felt. Could I make good this time? I had never followed through on a meaningful love affair. Take Cecily for example, how much I loved her, yet our relationship could not be called romance even in a stretch. And Casey whom I thought would be the love of my life nine years ago? That relationship ended when I traveled to Thailand and stayed there. Maybe I was escaping intimacy. And now Aida. How do I do this right? How do I enjoy and nurture the love I can never replace as long as I live, and not regret the sidelining of my talent, caring for the poor and needy? And what about making my life worth while?

The next day I decided to take Cecily's advice. I'd better find my creativity here before my trip to Copperhill.

I packed up my easel and acrylics, a few canvases. I packed jars to fill with seawater, rags and paper towels. I was going to paint the town of Seaside as it was now after the tsunami, looking up from the beach at the town.

I did get excited about what I saw that day. The sand had been cleared off of the boardwalk. Its old wooden planks took on a unique dimension, not only in my imagination. Most of the wood was raw. They had not been repainted in white. Maybe never would be. Looking up from them, the bright sun sparkled on the aluminum of new structures all over town. I tried to catch the recovery in my painting.

I returned home carefully carrying my newly wetted canvas. Cecily wasn't home yet but I knew she would be happy to see that I had taken her advice so I propped my 16 x 36 up on the back of the sofa where she would see it when she walked in the door. I pictured that, the way I had captured the sun glistening on the new aluminum in town, would make her blue eyes sparkle when she saw it. I took Romeo for a walk and picked up the mail on my way back into my condo.

That was the day the letter came. It was the letter I will remember until the day I die. How is my life different now because of that letter? That letter forced me to make a decision. It was in a plain business envelope with a regular forty-four cent postage stamp cancelled in Portland and forwarded to Seaside. If it hadn't been incorrectly addressed in the first place, I would have thought it was junk mail and thrown it away without opening it. But the forwarding made me study it closer, and open it. It was addressed to me, Aubrey Gentile by name on Seaside Street in Portland, with the return address that said simply, UNICEF. How did the post office know that the Aubrey Gentile who was addressed on the envelope lived in Seaside, Oregon, not Seaside Street in Portland? I think I had my fame, as a 'person of interest' in a serial murder, to thank for that.

The content of the letter was also far too simple for the import of its implications in my life:

Mr. Aubrey Gentile,

Sir:

UNICEF is looking for a nurse to fill a position in the town of Fagatogo, American Samoa. The person qualified for this position will have some experience in developing countries and a desire to live in this setting. Experience in treatment of tropical diseases, management of personnel and program development are also highly desirable. Please respond to this search by email providing educational references , job references and information regarding relevant experience. Email address follows.

Was this the answer to my search? It felt like I was being called. My previous experience was being recognized. If I accepted this challenge I would be working again in a setting with which I was familiar. I would have new challenges. I would be paid by the World Health Organization, not forty dollars a month this time, but enough to allow me to save toward my older retirement years. How could I not say 'yes' to this search?

I fired back a response.

I am interested in this position. Educational and job references to follow. I have experience in all the areas you are seeking.

What about Aida? I was being pulled in both directions as if I was on a rack, One leg was being pulled toward Aida, the other toward Fagatogo, literally half way around the world from each other. I couldn't wait for Cecily to arrive home. I knew she wanted me to continue my relationship with, and maybe marry Aida, but she could be honest with me as she had been yesterday. Was I truly more fit for foreign assignments than for a cozy wife and home? I wouldn't let Cecily just say I was escaping. I needed an honest critique based on her experience of me. I had no one else to ask for this help. Aida would say, "don't go," and if I still had Seamus Geary, he would say, "Go, get out of here."

I was full of anticipation, waiting to discuss my visit to Aida, the painting I had done this day, the letter from UNICEF, god, my whole future was there in front of me, waiting for a decision.

But, when Cecily arrived she stepped heavily into the doorway with this blank expression on her face even forgetting to close the door behind her. Romeo jumped up and down in front of her like a jumping jack, as he always did, without actually touching her. She usually grabbed him under his front legs and hugged him vigorously and laughed at him while he responded by licking her ears beneath her blond wedge followed by both of them nosing each other. This time she said, "no Romeo," and turned left and walked to her room without a word, followed by her confused but perceptive dog. She hadn't even noticed my great artwork.

After a long fifteen minutes she came back into the living room having changed into her jeans and black tee and said, "My mom called."

"What's wrong Cecily, is it your dad?" I asked.

"No. She said she had a call yesterday from a man by the name of Robert Ainsley. He told her he is from Eugene, Oregon but is now living in Chicago, studying at the Art Institute. He is twenty-one years old and is searching for his biological parents. His search so far has led him to the surname James, then to my parents."

"Cecily! It's Bobby! Bobby has found you! Why the glum face?" I asked.

"What did your mom say to him?"

"She told him she has a daughter in Seaside, Oregon who is single and has no children. She told him she'd discuss his call with her daughter and he should call her back in a week."

Now Cecily broke down into a sobbing so deep that it felt like it was coming from the center of the earth. Between jerky gasps she said, "What if we've lost him? What if he doesn't call again?"

I moved over and sat next to Cecily and put my arm around her shoulder. "He will try again. Call your mom back and tell her that she can give him your contact information. Let her know that you want her to tell him honestly, that you had a son and would welcome a call from him."

Cecily cried so hard, then interrupted her own tears and sobs, "I'm so happy he's okay. I'm sure he's had a good life or he wouldn't be there in Chicago now studying Art.

"How can I ever learn all I want to know about twenty-one years? How can I tell him I'm sorry. How can I make it up to him?"

"He will be grateful to you, Cecily, you won't have anything to make up."

"Why didn't my mom tell him to call me? How can I wait a whole week to find out if its him?"

"Maybe you won't have to wait," I said. She didn't tell him to call you because she doesn't know what you would want. You've been so distant from your parents. How do they know? Your mom and dad will help you. You'll see."

After that conversation, how could I bring up my painting and my visit to Aida? My letter? Suddenly the things that were my whole life a few minutes ago, were so unimportant. How could I talk about myself? Cecily blew her nose and wiped her eyes and calmed herself. She said that she needed to go for a walk on the beach and kick around a little sand and water. She wanted to be alone. While she was gone I took my painting of the town into my bedroom figuring I would show it to her another time. When she returned she went over to the television without a word and turned to "West Wing", on Netflix. She didn't watch for long but got up and paced around the apartment every few minutes, obviously not paying much attention to the story. She tried unsuccessfully to get her mind off of her son Bobby and her parents and her loss…and her hope.

CHAPTER 21

I **went back to work** in the emergency room without telling Cecily about the letter but a decision was eating at me. I couldn't discuss this with Aida online or on the phone. She was excitedly awaiting my visit just as I had been awaiting hers when she suddenly had taken on a daughter and cancelled her visit. I was painfully aware of how bad I felt at that time. I had to make a decision and inform her in person sometime before I left her, sometime while I was in Copperhill. I made a reservation on Delta for a flight to Chattanooga for October nineteenth, a week away.

Cecily called her mom as I had suggested. Her mom gave her Bobby's phone number and graciously suggested that they might work out a date to meet at the Oklahoma farm, all together. Her parents were so excited to be able to participate in this event. Cecily was afraid. "How do I even speak to my parents in person? It has been freezing cold between us for all of these years," she said.

"Cecily, you need to visit your mom first so that you can lessen the hard feelings that have developed between you and your parents. This is not a time to worry about who caused the icicles. You all will have to work at melting them and I know you can do your part. Your parents want to forgive you. That's what you have to do to. You don't want Bobby to have to deal with your heartache during your first visit with him. Maybe someday you can tell him about it, about how badly you wanted to keep him, and that you yourself were really just a child," I counseled.

"Aubrey, I don't even know yet if this is Bobby or some other Robert Ainsley. I'm waiting for my conversation with him and his adoptive parents first. I'm not even thinking about it, not giving myself hope. I wouldn't be able to stand it if it turns out not to be him."

Cecily did call Bobby and with his permission and encouragement, she called his parents. All of the dates and locations matched her history, born June first in Portland, Oregon, adopted June second, 1997 in a private, closed adoption and the kicker, father undetermined, mother Cecily James, information that had been sealed until recently. Robert Ainsley of Eugene, Oregon and now a twenty year old student at the Art Institute of Chicago was Cecily's son.

Cecily planned to drive to Eugene this week and visit the home where her Bobby had grown up, hear all the stories she could absorb about his childhood and tell her own stories to his parents. During that time I would stay with Romeo.

I knew that when she arrived home from Eugene her mind would be so full of the visit with the Ainsleys, that again I would not be able to discuss with her the letter from UNICEF and my own decision. I had to tell her now. As important as my decision was to me, I knew that she could not focus on me. Yet I had to let her know. What if my date of departure for Fagatogo was soon, even before Thanksgiving? She couldn't count on my help with Romeo. And maybe she needed time to prepare for losing her Seaside best friend: Me. She had told me that I was the closest she's ever had to a best friend in Seaside.

So I told her about my letter as casually as I could, to get it out of the way, while she was making after work snacks for both of us.

"Cecily, when you get back from the Ainsleys I'll be leaving the next day to visit Aida," I said.

"Do you think you'll come back here? Maybe you and Aida will make this permanent," she said. Cecily was way ahead of me with this suggestion.

"Something else has happened that I have not yet told you about," I said. "I received a letter last week from UNICEF. They're searching for a nurse to work in American Samoa."

"Permanently? But what about Aida?" she asked.

"Permanently. I'm leaning toward applying for the position. I'm really pretty sure about this right now. It seems like it's an answer to my questions about where I should live and work. Since the tsunami in Seaside and losing my job, I just don't seem to fit here as I thought I might," I said.

"But I'll always want to come back here to visit you. I can't discuss this opportunity with Aida from a long distance. We've gotten too close for that. I have to be there with her to tell her about it in person. Either way, Aida or Fagatogo, I probably won't be staying in Seaside for long."

"Maybe Aida would want to go to Samoa with you," Cecily offered.

"I don't think so. It's too poor there. I know what it's like to live in poverty. I couldn't ask her to subject Jahanara to that. Her child just found a stable life. She needs to grow up with a mother's attention, not more disruption."

"And a father's attention, Aubrey. She needs a father too," Cecily added. "What about how much she needs you?"

"Aida can find someone else. I can't make a decision about my life and Aida's life just because the child needs a dad."

"I know Aida's interest in you is not just for Jahanara's sake," she said. Aida was planning to visit you even before she knew about the child. Aida loves you Aubrey. If you'd rather go back to the life you lived for the last eight years, then go," She bristled. "Why did you come back to the States anyway?"

"Maybe I came back just to be sure...I need to contribute to life. To do something that will 'make the world a better place.' The people in a poor village need what I have to offer, more than people here."

"What happened to your philosophy that it's just as important to make people laugh or give them a good vacation or discover a star or see from a child's point of view? What about that, Aubrey? Maybe your life needs to match your philosophy better," she said. "That's what you call integrity."

"It's not all that simple," I said.

"Well maybe it should be. Maybe you should follow your heart for once, not just your head," Cecily said.

I knew I shouldn't have discussed this with Cecily right now. She was probably more acutely aware than ever, of her own loss, during all these twenty years since she had signed the papers that gave Bobby to someone else. I knew that, boiling up inside of Cecily, was the knowledge that she had foregone love and family as a punishment to her parents. She was feeling an emptiness that only she could allow to be filled. As she faced this pain, and she would do so bravely, she couldn't stand the idea of me giving up a family when I had a choice.

And how could anyone who hadn't lived my experience understand the pull that it had on me. When I found a job in Memory Care I thought I might have found in those people with Alzheimer's Disease and their families, the spiritual equivalent of the poor and needy in Muang Iai. But that Unit was gone now and with it my job, my opportunity to make life better for the residents and staff. I couldn't just run around the country looking for equivalents.

The next morning Cecily left early for Eugene.

"Cecily, are you excited?" I asked as I walked with her to the truck.

"My hands are sweaty, I'm afraid my feet won't stay still on the gas peddle and I'm having a bad hair day. Other than that, I am excited and happy. I wonder what the Ainsleys are like. If I don't like them this will be a tough visit, but I know I'll like them. They raised Bobby and he's a good person. I know he is, so they must be."

Cecily talked too much, for her. Just nervousness I was sure.

"Good. Your hair is gorgeous, but watch out for those feet dancing on that gas peddle. When you meet Bobby's family and hear the stories about him, when you see the home where he grew up, you're going to know that you did the right thing twenty-one years ago. It's going to be very painful to know what you've missed. But remember, it'll be like giving birth. All of that pain will soon be yesterday and it will turn into the happy you and especially, into the happy Bobby. You're going to have a new family and maybe also you'll have your original family back.

"Go now and don't even look at your phone for the next three days. Absorb every minute of this trip."

Cecily jumped into her truck and opened the window to stick her head out and wave as she backed out. She pulled away from the driveway with a screetch.

After waiving her off, as soon as the truck had turned the corner, I went to my computer. I composed my more detailed letter to UNICEF:

I am responding to your search for a nurse to serve in Fagatogo, American Samoa. My name is Aubrey Gentile. I am a registered nurse and have a master's degree in Geriatric Nursing. I am thirty-six years old and have lived the last eight years in Muang Iai, Thailand nursing people with tropical and poverty driven diseases. Since returning to the United States I have been employed as Manager of the Memory Care and Rehabilitation Units of Providence Hospital in Seaside, Oregon. These units were destroyed in the recent tsunami that hit our area after the Iliamna, Alaska earthquake. I am currently nursing in the emergency room of the same facility. My references follow.

I listed my nursing education At the University of Central Oklahoma, My Master's Degree in Geriatrics from UCLA, a letter from Brother Philip at the clinic in Muang Iai that I had used when I was hired by Dr. Geary and a reference from Providence Hospital with a footnote about Dr. Geary who hired me and was since deceased.

I studied my letter over and over for the three days that Cecily was gone. I was afraid to hit "Send". I couldn't hit it. I turned off the computer for fear that if it was open I might accidently hit "Send". What if I sent my letter and I was accepted? Maybe acceptance would be "a sign from God." I didn't want that sign. I had to tell Aida. Dare I? I tried not to imagine the look in her eyes, loss and forgiveness and anger all within their blackness. My answer lay in Copperhill, Tennessee. Answering a call by UNICEF would be painful. These were the circling thoughts that were creating my uncertainty.

Each of the next three days was about a hundred hours long. Finally I heard a truck pull up in front of the house. I looked out and saw that it was the blue Ram. Would Cecily be elated or a wreck when she walks in the door, I wondered. I had to be prepared for either. No matter what, this day had to be hers, not mine, and I was leaving in the morning for Copperhill. Tomorrow would be October nineteenth, the day before Jahanara's new birthday. I ran into the bedroom where my laptop was and, without re-reading my response to UNICEF for the umpteenth time, I hit "Send."

Cecily walked in the door humming and smiling. She was elated. Before she could tell me all about her visit she grabbed her stack of mail and flipped through it checking all the return addresses before opening any of it. She chose the envelope that looked like a genuine letter, not junk mail or business. It had no return address.

She opened it and read the card inside, read it again. "Aubrey, look," she reached it out for me to read. "A formal invitation from my parents for Thanksgiving Day Dinner at their home with the guest of honor, Mr. Robert Ainsley."

Cecily's eyes sparkled with wetness. "Aubrey, I can't stand all this happy news at once. What do I say?"

"Of course you say 'yes', I said."

"But why is it so formal?" she asked me.

"Because of your history with your parents. Your mom loves you so much, Cecily, wants so badly for you to come home, and she's scared too like you are," I said. "Cecily, call her. Tell her about your visit with the Ainsleys. Then ask her if you can come a few days before Thanksgiving and get to know her again before Bobby arrives. It's time Cecily. You have your son back, your parents need their daughter."

She did call home. She was on the phone with her parents forever. First she told her mom the whole story of her visit to the parents of Bobby Ainsley, her son. Then she told the whole thing again to her Dad. By the end of the phone call, what had started out to be hesitant and business like conversation had turned into a warm and hearty parent/daughter connection.

I knew then that life had changed forever for Cecily. She would now be able to have a real conversation with her parents about pain and forgiveness and about how they never again want to lose their connection with each other. I could picture her parents on the sheep farm in Broken Bow, Oklahoma, sobbing their hearts out after they hung up the phone. I heard the whole story again, the third time, of her visit to Eugene, just as told to her parents. When she hung up after her conversation with them, she told the story to me as if I had not yet heard it. The stories matched precisely. This was a profound time for Cecily, something she had been waiting for for twenty years and yet dared not allow herself to hope for. We just basked in her soul-stirring quiet for a long time. Before going to bed, I promised to be back from Copperhill long before Thanksgiving so that she could count on me to take Romeo while she went home for Thanksgiving.

"Romeo and I are planning to ride together in the Ram," she said. "We won't need you. Romeo will love the farm. My parents promised to let him be an inside dog while we are there but I have a hunch he'll be in training, learning to herd the sheep."

It was our last conversation before I left for Aida's. In the morning I awoke just in time to head for the airport where I would leave my Bug in long-term parking. I had packed the car the night before. I had too much luggage for the overhead compartment and would have to pay to carry it. Aida said that if I intended to paint I should bring what I would need because painting supplies are hard to get in her area. I also bought a two-foot tall stuffed Doberman for Jahanara's birthday present. These two things I could not do without. Cecily tried to get me to eat something before leaving but I insisted that I'd have plenty of time at the airport if I was hungry. She handed me a travel mug of coffee for the car, I kissed her quickly and headed out.

Cecily called out to me as I pulled the car away from the curb, "Aubrey, don't lose Aida." I didn't answer.

CHAPTER 22

***B*ecause I was flying from Portland into a smaller airport** I was one of the few passengers to be transported on a KLM Royal Dutch Airlines Douglas DC 3, a shiny silver narrow body plane with royal blue trim. This plane was very like its ancestor built in 1936. It had been sold to Delta for use between smaller airports and had stopped over in Portland, part of a world advertising tour, on its way from The Netherlands to Chattanooga where it would be based. What a treat that flight was! We flew smoothly at 32,000 feet most of the way. Portland was covered with thick grey clouds that morning but when the plane burst through them it was a sight to behold. Suddenly the light-filled white clouds were below the plane, dazzling, and dazzling too was the snow-covered pinnacle of Mount Hood. In fact the brilliance of that peak would have been masked by the clouds except for its linear shape, and the ragged purple lines of shade made by crevices lining and disrupting the mirror-like mountain slope. Shadows below the tree line looked like pencil marks but in fact were drawn by massive evergreens.

What could The One be like who conceived of and created this beauty? God has to Be Beauty, has to Be Love and Goodness if this amazing world is an extension of this God.

In my younger years I had been taught about a God who loved me if I was good, who won my baseball games if I prayed hard enough, who made some people well but not others, who kept me out of car crashes and tsunamis but allowed others to suffer them, who demanded the tortured death of a good and holy son to save the rest of us. Did God choose not to protect my parents or Seamus or Jaum? If Jahanara's beauty came from God, then someone else's deprivation also must have been from God. The God I know now has to be better than that.

This creation, first a big bang, exploding gas, then stars, light, heat, water, clouds, then life: plant life, animal life, human life. We have received an original blessing from the God I know, from the God Aida reminded me about. We have been given the power to use the blessing of existence, for ourselves and others. The God I know is in this world as us, as everyone, as everything that is.

What was I thinking when I considered my UNICEF letter as a call? a sign? As if someone was answering my question for me, telling me what choice to make. Whatever decision I make would be blessed because I'm free to do what I choose. I can't blame someone else or circumstances or a 'call.' I have the ability to make wise choices, to know myself and choose what is best for me and for those I love. This decision would be my burden and my privilege, not God's.

Douglas 3 and I were just five hours from Aida and still I was leaning toward accepting a UNICEF job opportunity. Why? I would be open to Aida's wisdom and love, to the beauty and needs and opportunities of Copperhill and I would not blame God or circumstances or anyone else for my choice. It wasn't a question of what God wants, but what I want. I felt free. I knew that no choice would remove a God who wraps Godself around all of this universe including me. This God is with me in all my good and poor choices. In all circumstances.

When I deplaned, lovely Aida was at the airport, right up in front of the crowd holding Jahanara by the hand. Aida had no inhibitions like I had had when waiting for her plane to arrive in Portland. She stretched her arms out to receive me into them, looked into my eyes longingly and bent her head back ever so tenderly to receive my kiss on her lips. Jahanara at her side jumped up and down all the while saying "Oh Me, Oh Me!" I bent down and hugged and kissed her too.

"Welcome to Tennessee and welcome home," Aida said warmly. The airport was too cool, but I didn't care. It felt like I was home. Outside it was still warm, about seventy degrees and sunny. Fall was in the colors but not yet in the air. Aida, black hair still in her French braid, was wearing a white cardigan sweater over a black and white checked fitted blouse, black jeans and again, a yellow flower in her hair. She wore no makeup, her lips and cheeks were pink, her skin was olive, her eyes were bright and lashes long without makeup. Jahanara wore yellow bibbed jeans and a white blouse and sweater. Both of them were beaming, radiant.

"We have a long drive ahead of us," Aida said. Let's get your luggage and get on the way. The drive is about two and a half hours but it would be fun to stop at a country café on the way if you're not too hungry to wait. The road is winding and hilly and the green is turning all gold and orange and red right now. There is only one lane each direction all the way. Stopping along the way helps me concentrate on this road better."

Aida had a red Honda Fit, plenty big for the three of us. I opened the rear to place my luggage. Aida jumped in front of me to throw a tarp over the dirt in the back before loading my things.

"Oh, I'm so sorry for the dirt," she said. "I carried a lot of mums in the back of the car yesterday, for the gardeners to plant on the island down the center of Main street in Blue Ridge. We'll drive over there for you to see Blue Ridge, Georgia sometime this week. You can see my work there and we'll sit in the gazebo and have lunch.

Aida was excited about her home area. She was ready to give me all the tourist propaganda before we could even get on our way.

"The town of Blue Ridge is very pretty and sophisticated for a mountain town. It's the tourist area, a lot busier and has a lot more money than Copperhill. There is so much for people to do there, river boating, kayaking, fishing. There is a huge finger lake and a dam built by the Tennessee Valley Authority. You can hike through woods with numerous waterfalls almost wherever you go. The Appalachian Trail begins just south of there near the town of Elijay and goes for two thousand miles into the State of Maine."

Now I could see for myself why she loved the area so much. Along the road were small tourist sites, like kayak rental and bait shops where fishing licenses were sold. After about an hour's drive Aida pulled into a small café parking spot with parking for about four vehicles. It was surrounded by golden trees and we could hear the Ocoee River water rustling behind the cafe. We asked to be seated there by the water, at an outdoor wrought iron table. Its umbrella was folded closed, giving us a full view of the trees on the other side of the water. Jahanara wanted an egg salad sandwich which she called a "sanich" and Aida and I both ate salads. All the vegetables were homegrown by the café owner's family members. I told Aida I needed photos to copy from when I painted. I took the pictures with my cell phone, lots of pictures, pictures of the trees, pictures of the river and café, pictures of us together. If I didn't return I would at least have pictures for memories.

We pulled into Copperhill just as the sun was setting behind the purple ridges above Main Street. The homes rose steeply between town and the ridge. The street was almost empty of traffic except at the A & P, parking lot, the town's main supermarket. The population of Copperhill was three hundred fifty-four and all the people I think, were at the A & P. We stopped at the middle of the town's three stoplights right in front of the store.

"Look over there," Aida said, pointing to the parking lot. "See that yellow line down the center of the lot? It marks the division between the State of Tennessee and the State of Georgia." She pointed up the hill behind the store. I could barely see what she was indicating because of the setting sun glaring in my eyes. "I live on the second street from the top. The farther you are from town the more space you can have for a yard and I wanted a yard so I had to sacrifice the convenience of being on level land."

Then she said almost dreamily looking into my eyes, "Let's go home."

Aida navigated the streets that headed up at a forty-five degree angle with no difficulty and pulled into the driveway at the side of her home on Dogwood Drive. The little frame two-story house was painted yellow with white trim. Lights were on shining through all the windows. Window boxes in the front were full of pansies of all colors. The wooden front porch was unpainted rickety wood, the front yard facing town was almost too small to count as a yard. It was almost entirely filled with the trunk and roots of a fully-grown maple tree. The back yard facing the top of the hill was large and fenced with chain links. It had a level lawn, lots of grey and reddish rocks setting apart small areas within it and it had a weeping willow tree.

"One of these days I'm going to work on this yard," Aida said. "I'm so busy doing landscape design for a business that I never take care of my own. It will be a great place for you to sit and paint though, even without the flowers, but someday we'll have flowers back here."

CHAPTER 23

Aida wanted to enter the house through the back door. I grabbed my luggage while she opened the gate and Jahanara skipped along the walk to the back door.

"This house was built at the turn of the century, 1900, not 2000," Aida said. Copper mining was big in this area at that time and this was probably considered a luxury house then, since this town was mostly populated by miners. I had to have all the plumbing and electric work newly done when I bought it about eight years ago, but I kept the old wooden floors and the quaint chandeliers. The first time this house had an air conditioner unit was the one I had installed. The windows are new too, but they are the same style as the old ones that were replaced."

The main floor had a kitchen with an octagonal breakfast room just big enough for a forty-eight inch round table. It had surrounding arched French windows. And surely enough, the chandelier. This one was wrought iron with five candle shaped bulbs.

The formal dining room had a brown wooden table, china cabinet and sideboard, dainty in style and probably about the same age as the house... must have always been where it was now. The chandelier was wrought iron like the one in the breakfast nook but larger and more ornate and hung low over the table. An archway led from the dining room into the living room. The living room was small and warm with a wood burning fireplace on one side. It was furnished with a tan overstuffed leather sofa with matching chair, rough wooden coffee table and wooden side chairs. There was a bathroom too on the main floor with an old iron tub, blue and white octagonal nickel size tiles on floor and lower wall and built in white three-drawer cabinet and mirror. Finally on the first floor there was a little nook that was totally filled by Aida's desk, computer and printer.

The upstairs had three bedrooms, one for Aida with a double bed, one for Jahanara with a single white child's bed and one for a guest...me? This was going to be difficult. When would I make my move to Aida's room, or would I?

There was a second bathroom on that floor with both shower and tub, and bathtub toys on a little wicker table next to the tub. "My things," Jahanara said proudly holding up a rubber duck. A second bathroom was a luxury at the time this house was built and this house had three, as a later owner had installed one in the basement.

The basement was finished for a laundry, play room and T.V. room. Aida noted that she didn't have to worry about flooding in her basement since the house was built so near the top of a steep hill. That assured full use of the basement.

"Tomorrow's my birthday," Jahanara told me on the way back to the main floor. "I'm going to be four."

"I know, I said. "I brought you a present. Should I give it to you now?"

"No," she said emphatically. "Mamada said you are my birthday present. I want you to be my present."

I opened the big brown paper package I had carried along with my suitcase and pulled out the Doberman as she watched, full of excitement. When she saw it she raised both arms to the sky. "Romeo," she exclaimed. "Can I have both presents?"

"Yes, you can have Romeo to keep, and you'll always have my visit to remember," I said. I was being careful not to promise her that she could have me to keep.

"Can Romeo sleep with me? she asked.

"Of course he can. He's yours to keep now. You can take care of him, sleep with him, do anything you want with him," I said.

Aida took Jahanara up to her room, got her into her three bear flannel pajamas and into her bed. Then she called me to come upstairs to tuck her in. By the time I put Romeo under the covers to snuggle with her, promised to be there when she woke up in the morning and kissed her goodnight on the forehead, she was on the verge of sleep.

I returned downstairs to Aida and found that she had started a fire in the fireplace. There were no other lights on in the living room but I could see Aida sitting on the sofa waiting for me. She was still fully dressed.

"Come on over here and sit by me," she said, motioning to me to sit beside her. She had opened her braid and was running her fingers through her long wavy hair, pulling out the braid.

I sat close to Aida, electricity ran quivering through my entire body wanting to absorb hers into mine. I put my arm around her shoulder. She fit perfectly into me, each of her concave curves matching my convex ones. I kissed her lightly on the lips and looked into her eyes to see what she was wanting next. Aida kissed me too and suddenly we were entwined. Like a ficus tree whose two trunks have grown around and into each other all of its life, we almost could not be separated. Aida's leg was over my lap, her hair was soft and smelled clean like freshly ironed cotton as it fell across my face. I cupped her small soft breasts while she reached between the buttons of my shirt and stroked my chest. We kissed each other all over our faces and ears and eyes.

Then she pulled back from me slightly. I felt her shying away. I did not want to rush her, to lose the feel of her softness. I wanted her to know my gentleness but I was overpowered by my raging need of her. I quieted myself to honor her lead. "I have to talk to you, Aubrey." There's something we have to talk about before we continue this."

I kept my arm around her and sat, still close, catching my breath, watching the fire and listening to its crackle. I composed my self for a minute, as she too was doing.

As she spoke and I replied, we continued to massage each other's thighs, sending the message of our long awaited intimacy, even without knowing we were doing so.

"Okay," I finally said, "What do you need to say?"

"Aubrey, before we get so absorbed in each other that we can't make good decisions, we need to know where our relationship is going. I love you so much. I've been hoping that having some time together this week, would help us know each other well, to be sure of ourselves. But here we are. Already we can't wait to belong completely to each other, and you just got here."

I tried to think about what she was saying and respond to her need, but I was already past the thinking part. I said, "Aida, you were with me during and after the tsunami. We had two life-changing weeks together. It was one of the most difficult times in my life. I feel that we already do know each other pretty well."

"Let me talk," Aida said, "before I lose my courage. Here's what I have to tell you. I've had a job offer in Chicago. It sounds like a wonderful opportunity for me. I'll tell you more about it later, but here's the thing. If it was just myself, I would jump at the chance to do this. But it's not just me now. You and I have found each other. We're both in our late thirties. We've waited a long time and it seems like we both have found everything we've been waiting for. I can't just think about me now."

She paused and I kissed her again on the lips, urgently. She returned my kiss but got back to the conversation she felt the need to complete.

"I have found you," she continued. "I'm sure you could find work in Chicago but would you want to? It's not the kind of life you love. It's not lush like Seaside and you wouldn't be part of a native culture there like the one you had in Thailand. I don't want our love for each other to force either of us into a life that doesn't fit our dreams."

I had not intended to discuss UNICEF so soon, I had wanted to experience life with Aida for most of the week before bringing up the possibility of losing each other. But she had walked me right to the crossroads. I had to tell her now. Had to let her put this into the equation of her life as well as mine.

"Aida, I too have something I need to share with you. I didn't want to discuss it now, tonight. I wanted a love fest before doing the hard part, but…This is so difficult."

I could see the questioning look, the fear in her eyes, the thought that she was about to lose me.

"Aida, I received a recruitment letter from UNICEF offering me an interview for a position in American Samoa. I fit all of their requirements to a tee. I am the perfect candidate and if I say yes, it is almost surely my position. I will never have a chance like this again.

This offer is a recognition of all the work I've done for almost a decade of my life."

"Oh Aubrey," she said with a tremor in her voice while shaking her head "no". . "You would be so happy there. I think you would feel fulfilled again, like it was what you were meant for. I love you too much to take this from you. If that's what you want you must do it. If you do, then I should take the job in Chicago. It would be a brand new venue for me, and an adjustment for Jahanara, but we can do it."

"Aida, tell me more about the Chicago job," I said.

"I would be responsible for designing the landscaping in all the city parks, assuring that each one has substantial nature preserve areas. People would be using parks to experience countryside and nature rather than just playing sports and using swings. This job would have a future in it for me, doing the work that I love. I was offered an interview there in two weeks. If you are leaving me, I'd better make an appointment for the interview."

We sat silently watching the fire for the next twenty minutes. Every now and then I would pull Aida closer. She would look up at me and give me a tiny tortured tremoring smile, reach up with her trembling lips and kiss me lightly, but both of us were afraid to engage each other fully again or to again open up this conversation. The fire slowly turned to coals, then embers and the room started to cool down. Finally Aida said, Why don't you bring your bags upstairs. You'd better take the guest room for now. I think it's better for you to sleep in there for tonight.

"Of course," I said, my head and heart strongly disagreeing with each other.

We both headed up the stairs. We stopped at the door to my bedroom and kissed goodnight quickly and lightly. Bravely. As Aida turned away toward her room I turned into mine. Then I looked back and saw that she too, was looking back. When we saw the desire in each other's eyes we turned and stepped slowly, first one step, then two steps, until we could not be stopped by the dam, but rushed into each other's embrace. We found together that night, what we had both been hungering for. We became one. It was like diving head first into the waiting water, not just the deep end of a pool but into the raging sea. We were fully immersed and carried away into the violent, cool, passionate waves of the sea.

When we both awoke in the midnight stillness, I was carried once more, but this time effortlessly into Aida's waiting, welcoming softness.

CHAPTER 24

When I awoke about seven it was to Jahanara's voice, Aida was gone. "Oh Me, wake up," she said, jumping up on the bed. "Today is my birthday and you are my present."

"Happy Birthday, Joy," I said, trying to open my eyes all the way while stretching my arms and frame. "What are we going to do today?" I asked her.

"You have to come downstairs and eat breakfast," she said.

So I got dressed and obeyed. When I got downstairs Aida was flipping pancakes. I put my arm around her and kissed her as naturally as if we had been doing this for a long time, but again I experienced quivers, desire. Jahanara was sitting on her high chair riding it like a horse. "Mamada said you could take me to see the dogs, for my birthday," she said.

I could see then that these days would be a chance for Aida and I to know and share each other better. We would not be focusing on a disaster, digging through mold, consoling everyone except ourselves like we had during her visit to Seaside. Here I would be spending the day with a child while aching for more of Aida. I didn't like pancakes but I was getting to experience one of the compromises that are an inevitable part of ordinary days together.

Later I would be seeing where Aida works and how she works. I would be seeing the town where she lives, the people she shares time with, the way she parents. In this place I knew that Aida was not on stage, she was just her real gentle self. If I would just relax and enjoy the time together Aida could see me too, find my flaws as well as 'how great I am'.

"Aubrey, this morning I have to finish up the work I was doing downtown Blue Ridge before you came. Then I think I can take the rest of the week off. If you want to ride to Blue Ridge with me, you and Jahanara can do some things in town while I'm working. She wants you to take her to the dog shelter for her birthday. I can show you how to get there and you can take the car while I'm working."

So our first day was taken care of, planned. The road from Copperhill to Blue Ridge was two-lanes wide. It was guarded on both sides by ivy-covered rock cliffs. The trees were turning bright colors, alternating with green. Lacy hemlock interrupted the shiny ivy just as along the road from Chattanooga. After receiving directions from Aida and dropping her off downtown Blue Ridge, my assignment included a visit to the dog shelter of Blue Ridge. This was a newly built facility which had kennels for fourteen dogs and all of them were occupied.

The gentleman volunteer at the front desk, Mr. Cooper, recognized Jahanara right away. "Well look who's here. My little Joy!" he said.

She ran around the counter to give him a hug and he squatted so that she could reach him. "It's my birthday," she said. "Can I visit the dogs?"

"Of course you can," Cooper replied.

Mr. Cooper assured me that it was safe for her to enter. Her mother brought her here regularly for visits so she knew how to safely approach the dogs. That darling child headed right for the largest, oldest dog. "Snoopy," she said with her arms up in the air. Then she squatted in front of his kennel and let him lick her hand. Mr. Cooper took us into the dogs' play yard and brought Snoopy out for us. Joy sat down on the ground for him just as she had done for Romeo and he came over to her and lay down in front of her, face to face. After their time together, talking with each other, I guess, Mr. Cooper allowed her to hold onto Snoopy's collar and walk him back to his kennel. She then walked past all of the other kennels and spoke to each dog, calling each by name, as in "Hi Porky," and "Baby Jane, you're my favorite dog." Then we left the shelter.

We met Aida back at the in town, bought take-out sandwiches at a deli and walked to the gazebo in the park-like strip that ran down the middle of Main Street. Aida had planned the landscaping of this park, which now displayed multiple fall colors except for the magnolia and pine trees that remained green. We walked up and down Main Street stopping at the tea store, the oil store, the pajama store and the Art store. I did the rest of the town with Jahanara as Aida returned to work to finish up her week.

By the time we returned to Aida's home in Copperhill the day was almost spent. Aida invited the teen babysitter from next door and the four of us sang happy birthday and ate cake and ice cream before taking Jahanara up to bed and tucking her in for the night.

I made a fire this time in the living room fireplace We sat cozily on the sofa again and talked. Aida wanted to know all about Cecily so I told her the whole story of Bobby, from his birth until now, how Cecily visited Bobby's adoptive parents and about the soul shaking moments that Cecily would still have to face.

I told her about the last three months since the tsunami, about how the town was resurrecting, how the boardwalk and lighthouse had survived a tsunami again, as they probably have many times since they were first built. I told her about the work I was doing in the emergency room, about the doubt I entertained that the Memory Care and Rehabilitation Units would be rebuilt. I told her how much I missed Seamus Geary. I told her about my talk with Cecily and my painting of the renewed town. I apologized for all the trauma that I had put her through after the tsunami hit.

"Why would you apologize for something you could do nothing about? Think of it as an experience very few people will ever have and so we are richer because of it. After all, how many hosts put on a tsunami to entertain their guests?" she laughed.

"One more thing, I said, the important thing, Tillie was finally arrested in Sequoia National Park just last week." I told her how sad I was about Tillie. I can only hope that, since California hasn't executed anyone since 2006, she may be safer in prison than out in public. I hope that she won't be executed. She and I shared a weird sort of friendship. I don't know if she can learn, but I can't wish to see her executed either.

The only thing I did not tell Aida about was what Cecily had said before I left, "Don't lose Aida."

The next day I wanted to spend at home with Aida. "Aida, can I help you with the work you want to do in your back yard? That would be so much fun for me on this sunny fall day."

"If we're going to work out there I have to run over to the nursery to get some of the things I want to plant," she said.

So I had my tour of Copperhill before we could get to work. Its main street is crossed by four other commercial streets. The live railroad track and the Ocoee River flow through town. There is an old iron rusty tall bridge over the river. It crosses the street which heads to a new Interstate several miles away. Aida especially wanted me to see the new enterprises that were giving so much hope to the people here. The new restaurant on the Ocoee River bank fit into the old landscape so beautifully. This café had it's own hiking trails around the grounds where waiting customers could hear their name called when their table was ready or could stroll after eating to wear off the new pounds they had just put on. Remodeling was happening all over town, a hopeful sign for current proprietors.

Our last stop was the new nursery in town. It not only sold seasonal flowers, trees and shrubs but also had educational signs around the walls displaying native species and nature's gifts: weed and insect species. The signs explain which plants benefit the environment and which do harm in this area.

We picked up Flame azaleas, crocus, iris and tulip bulbs, which Aida wanted to plant now, to be ready for blooming in early spring. We purchased small Trout lilies, a perennial wildflower with yellow blooms that would bloom now growing among the moss. Then we returned home to start digging, replacing and propping up the soil with fertilizer and manure.

Aida and I were getting to work, both of us had our hands deep in the rich, warm, soft soil when my phone rang. I shook the dirt off, rubbed my dirty hands on my jeans and grabbed my phone. It was Cecily.

"You have a letter here from UNICEF. I don't want to open it but I thought you would want to know it came," she said.

"Cecily, open the letter," I said nervously. No matter what it said I did not want it to ruin my time with Aida. But then, if I was turned down for the job, I could forget about Fagatogo and enjoy my time with her better. "Cecily, read it to me."

I could hear her tear the envelope open and I could hear the paper rustle as she unfolded the letter. All of my senses were more alert now like they are when you're in love or when you're deathly afraid. After the letter was open I heard a long pause.

"Cecily, what does it say?" I asked urgently.

"A representative from UNICEF will be in Seaside next week to review the projects, plans and repairs that were sponsored by the United Nations after the tsunami. Our representative would like to interview you for the position in Fagatogo, American Samoa while he is there.

I thanked Cecily for letting me know. I asked her to read to me the phone and email information from the letter so that I could set up the appointment. I turned off the phone without the banter or conversation that she and I would normally engage in. Of course Aida noticed. She must have seen that I was stunned.

"What's the matter, Aubrey?" she asked looking concerned.

"A letter came from UNICEF. They want me to interview for the job in Fagatogo. They want me to set up an appointment with a representative in Seaside for next week." We looked at each other without another word but both of us were shouting "no" with our eyes.

The birds stopped singing, the leaves stopped rustling, the flowers drooped and the worms crawled back into the mud. Aida dropped her hand-rake at her side. Like a robot I turned and walked across the yard. I filled the wheelbarrow with a mixture of manure and dirt and brought it back to the garden where I would plant some of the new Trout Lillies. I knelt back down on the earth and continued my work. After watching me for a few minutes and realizing I could not talk about the letter just now, Aida too, went back to her digging.

When we had worked several hours, Aida said to me, "I'd like to work a little longer but why don't you clean up and get out your paints. I think you need to take a break. Yard work is never done, you know. We've gotten a good start this morning."

"I'd love to do that," I said. "What I really want to do first is sketch Jahanara. I know she won't be able to sit still for me for long so I can't do her portrait all at once. If I start today, I'll have the rest of the week to work on that a little at a time. But don't clean her up first, I'll draw her just as she is with dirt on her cheeks and shirt, in the dappled light under the weeping willow."

"Jahanara, you help your mom while I go in to clean up. Then I want to draw a picture of you, Okay?"

I went up to my room to wash up and change into my shorts and a clean tee. Then I texted the telephone number I had been given for UNICEF *"In response to your letter of 10/17/17 I request an interview in Seaside, Oregon. I am available any day during your visit there. Please notify me of the time of the interview by response to this text. Thank You"* I hit "Send."

I gathered my painting supplies and sketch pad and charcoal and pencil and returned to the yard where Aida had already placed a stump under the willow for Jahanara to sit on. Sketching Jahanara took me out of 'robot mode,' and enabled me to focus. I spent the rest of the afternoon sketching her with frequent breaks for snacks and for her to run loose in the yard.

That evening as we sat again before the fire, Aida asked, "Do you want to talk about your appointment?"

"I don't know what to say," I said.

"Well Aubrey, I don't either," she said, "But I think you do know what you want. Deep down there in the depths of your soul, you know exactly what you want to do about your dilemma. I don't think it's right for me to try to influence you. When you're ready you'll tell me what you've decided and we'll go from there. If your plans include me I will be so happy. But if not, we can write to each other and call anyway, see what happens next."

"Aida, I could not ask you to wait, and joining me there is not an option. I think I am being asked by UNICEF to work in a primitive setting and you have Jahanara to think about now." I wasn't even leaving a crack in the door open for Aida to slip through. She had to know that if I was gone, she would be free to go wherever life takes her. I couldn't give my all to this assignment knowing she was waiting.

Aida called the high school girl next door who baby sits for Jahanara sometimes, and asked her to come over and do her homework while the baby slept.

"Let's go for a walk," Aida said to me. "I'll be quiet if you want to think or to tell me your thoughts about Fagatogo. I will always be grateful for the time we have together. Let's not waste a minute of it."

CHAPTER 25

It **was my fourth day** out of seven in Tennessee. No, I also did not want to waste another minute of my time with Aida. She was right. Deep down in the depths of my soul I knew exactly what I wanted to do, not just next week but for the rest of my life. It was as clear as that full moon had been on our walk last night, as Jupiter was, posted up there, neighbor to the moon. It was as clear as the filtered water falling over the dam, as beautiful and bright as the clouds around Mount Hood, as promising as tomorrow. 'I love you tomorrow'.

I begged the car from Aida and told her I had an errand in town. I'm sure she was curious about my errand but was considerate enough not to ask and I didn't tell her where I was going. She handed me the car keys without a word or question.

"I'm sure I'll be back by noon," I told her. Maybe you can figure out what we should do this afternoon. Anything is okay with me."

Among the new businesses opening up in Copperhill I had seen a travel agency. Knowing that I might have to make complicated arrangements quickly I went there for my tickets. I purchased three tickets for Chicago leaving Chattanooga on October thirtieth. I booked a hotel for a week near Millennial Park and the famous Art Museum. I cancelled my return trip ticket for Portland. That trip would have to wait. When all that was accomplished I texted the number I had been given for UNICEF, the same one I had used just yesterday to set up my appointment with them.

> *"Please cancel my appointment with your representative for next week in Seaside, Oregon. I will not be accepting the position in Fagatogo. Thank you for considering me. Sincerely, Aubrey Gentile*

Copperhill also had a new OfficeMax. I headed over there to make a paper copy of my response to UNICEF. I bought an envelope that had yellow flowers printed on the flap and put the copy of my note to UNICEF and the three plane tickets to Chicago inside.

I could move to Chicago. I could live anywhere Aida lived. I could not be happy again without Aida. I did not want her to be on the other side of the world, digging in the green earth, adding to its beauty without me. I did not want to miss seeing Jahanara turn five and then six and then seven and start school. I wanted someday to walk her up the aisle when she was joining her husband to be, the man who would equal, no surpass my love for her.

What would I do with this gift of life? I knew now for certain. I knew the second I hit "send" when I had made the appointment with UNICEF that I had made the wrong decision. What would I do with my wonderful life? I would dig in the earth with Aida and paint her outdoor creations in their bright purples and oranges and reds and give the paintings the spirit that she gave the landscape. And I would probably continue to nurse. I'd get a real nursing job, maybe home care or hospice, where I would be with people in their need. I knew now from experience that administration was not for me.

I couldn't wait to tell Aida of my decision but it had to be at the right time. Tonight when we're alone after Jahanara is tucked in bed, I'll tell her.

We all three went for dinner to the Ocoee River Café and ate the trout that we were told was caught that very day down by the riverside near the café. The tomatoes were homegrown and the apples in the dessert came from the owner's trees. I couldn't wait to get home and tuck Jahanara into bed again. This evening had to be ours, mine and Aida's. When I came back down to the living room this time there was no fire in the fireplace. Aida was standing out on the back porch and she called, "Come here Aubrey, I want to show you something." She pointed to the sky. She was getting ready for my decision.

It was late dusk. The red rays from the receding sun were now only a narrow streak on the horizon, but the clouds above it that had been white looked almost like fluffy rainbows, red at the bottom, then yellow above, then lavender and blue.

"I have a surprise for you," Aida said, "But I don't want to miss any of this sunset so I'll tell you as soon as it's dark."

"I have a surprise for you too," I told Aida.

"You have to go first," she said as soon as it was dark enough that only the white fence caught the moon reflection. We sat down on the back porch furniture and lit the yellow bug light.

"Okay," I said. I pulled out the envelope that I had prepared for Aida that morning and handed it to her.

"What's this?" she asked.

"Open it," I said. I watched her face intently as she carefully opened the envelope, trying to avoid tearing the yellow flowers. I expected something like a gasp and then *Oh Aubrey, I love you so.*

But Aida's face fell. She studied the plane tickets that she had dropped from the envelope onto the table. She looked bewildered, puzzled, tearful. She shook her head, "No! You can't! we can't go to Chicago! Besides, what about your appointment next week in Seaside?"

"Aida, I cancelled my appointment with UNICEF in Seaside. Read the paper there, my note to UNICEF. I copied it for you to save if you want to."

She continued to look silently confused so I asked her,

"What was your surprise for me, Aida? I realized she couldn't speak.

"That's just it," she said. She handed me a printout of her surprise. It was a reservation for three on Delta Airlines to Portland, Oregon for next Monday. "I cancelled your return flight so that we can all fly to Portland together. I want to come and be with you when you have your interview. In case you have to leave for your new job in Samoa soon, I'd have a little more time with you before you go if I'm already there. I cancelled my appointment in Chicago too. I turned down the position there. I decided that I don't want to be there alone without you."

We looked at each other both holding up the plane tickets that would never be used. We both had open mouths and wet eyes, were both shaking our heads "no" while gradually our heads changed from movements of no, to disbelief, to nods of "yes." "Yes!"

"But what about your 'call'? I don't want you to do this unless its what you really want to do and really know it's right for you," Aida said.

"Aida, I don't need a message. This is my miracle, to stand on this green earth with you and Jahanara at my side. I am totally and completely in love with you, Aida. The miracle is this. The Thai villagers taught me, when I stood at the riverside with them. We watched our flowers and candles float down their river and they said, 'life is about beauty, enlightenment, oneness and passage to eternity.' These things I have with you, Aida. If you will say 'yes' to me I will marry you and we will live wherever you choose. Wherever you go I will go."

"Yes, of course Yes," she said.

"Aida, will you wait here a minute? I have something I want to give you." I ran up the stairs two at a time to retrieve my gift. I had been saving it for the right moment. I did not have a ring for her but I had something so much more precious than a ring.

When I came back she said, "I was thinking, can I tell Jahanara that she has a Daddy now? Can we tell her in the morning?"

"Of course we can. She can call me Daddy and you Mama. She has one of each now. Maybe we can name her first dog, "OhMe. So we won't forget that precious name."

I handed Aida the yellow and pink Thai silk pasin that the villagers of Muang Iai had weaved and given me for my going away present. She unfolded the silk, eyes glistening. "It's beautiful," she said. "Where did you get it? Tell me about it."

I did tell her. I told her how the villagers all pitched in to create it. How some of them grew and fed the silk worms, how some of them boiled and pulled threads from the worms' cocoons. I told her about the klongs or canals where the threads were dyed and about the hand made looms that the men built without a nail. I told her how weavers worked hours and months to weave the yellow and pink threads into a plaid pattern and how proud they were when they presented it to me, and how poignant that moment was. Then I added, "Seeing you in this silk will be like having all the villagers smiling at you and me together and saying they want to be one with us."

"Aubrey, I told you I have never worn the Muslim hijab and it's true, I haven't, but do you think I could wear this as a hijab for our wedding? It would be such a powerful sign, like the flowering of our love for each other and for life."

Aida put the pink and yellow plaid Thai silk cloth over her head and wrapped it around her shoulders, pinching it under her chin as she looked up at me. The loose black strands of her hair that slipped from her French braid laced her face and picked up the shine of moonlight.

I once had had a dream, but it had not been this radiant.

CHAPTER 26

***Copperhill Call*, the town's weekly news** carried a quarter page ad for us the week before our wedding.

Aida Sadat of Copperhill, Tennessee and
Aubrey Gentile of Broken Bow, Oklahoma
request the honor of your presence at their wedding
at the Ocoee River Cafe'
at 2:00 in the afternoon
on November 30, 2018

As we hope all of our townspeople will be a part of our lives,
You are all welcome to celebrate with us the beginning of
our life together.

Please, No material gifts.

We saw no reason to wait for our wedding. We were completely committed to each other from the day of our betrothal. We had been waiting for thirty-six years for this to happen. We also had other commitments, both to Jahanara who already had claimed us as her parents and to Seamus, our son, to be named for Dr. Seamus Geary. He was now six weeks old in utero, having been conceived, we felt sure, on October nineteenth of this year, the night that I arrived in Copperhill.

Maybe not so coincidentally, the week long festival of Loi Krathong was being celebrated in Thailand the same week as our wedding in Copperhill.

It was not easy for our friends and family to get to Copperhill. They had to fly into Chattanooga or Knoxville, Tennessee or Atlanta, Georgia then drive at least two hours on winding, hilly, roads, sometimes with steep drops on the side of the road. This was not a trip for the weak, but they were all foolhearty enough.

Aida's Mother and Aunt Pari came for the wedding and stayed in our house for two weeks after the wedding to take care of Jahanara while we celebrated our honeymoon. Her brother Emil and his family could not come from Iran but sent a wonderful message, saying that they hoped we would always be as happy as they were together. They sent pictures of their family that we would cherish.

Cecily of course came and would be the primary witness of our vows. Since she and her son Bobby had been visiting Cecily's parents in Oklahoma over the Thanksgiving holiday, they were able to arrange for all four of them to travel to Copperhill for our wedding, by Ram truck, no less, bringing Romeo with them.

Uncle Oscar and his wife, my aunt Charlotte arrived stealthily the night before the wedding and stayed in the local Comfort Inn. I was totally flabbergasted to see them when I arrived at the Ocoee River Cafe' just before the wedding. I saw a gentleman standing around among the gathering guests who I noticed looked like Uncle Oscar. Of course it isn't him, I thought. Then I saw Cecily walk over to take him by the hand, laugh with him and bring him to me. When they approached, my gasp took most of the air out of my lungs and our hug finished me off. Of course, like always, he said the wrong thing, "Aubrey, I thought for sure it would be Cecily you'd marry. But I can't wait to meet the woman that you chose ahead of her. That must be some woman."

Having Oscar and Charlotte, my paternal uncle and his wife at our wedding was the next best thing to having my own parents there. It made our family and the congregation complete.

Cecily's son Bobby's parents whom of course I had never met, came to the wedding. Although they, the Ainsleys, didn't know either Aida or me, they were people who were always up for a good party. And they hoped to know us someday. They used this occasion to get to know the James family, Cecily and her parents. Cecily was

Bobby's birth mother, and her parents were his grandparents. They all, the James family and the Ainsley family had plans to vacation for a week in Blue Ridge, Georgia after the wedding.

How can I describe our wedding?

Somewhere in the range of two hundred of the townspeople, out of its total population of three hundred sixty, came to our wedding. The mood among them was as festive as Christmas and and Easter and July fourth all wrapped up together. They lined the walk from the cafe,' over the little wooden bridge and into the woods. The hum of happy conversation continued as Reverend Sarah and I took our places.

Sarah, a friend of Aida's and also a catholic priest was serving as the minister of our wedding vows. She and I stood waiting at the head of the garden walk at the entrance to the outdoor cafe'. I was dressed in full black tails but no one noticed. No one quieted or paid any attention to us until, from the other end of the crowd, our flowering four year old child led the procession out of the woods. Then the crowd stilled instantly and the music started.

Jahanara, with both hands, raised carefully, carried a lace pillow to which our golden wedding bands were tied. She wore a full skirted calf length dress of white lace over yellow taffeta, white shoes and white stockings. She had a yellow and white frangipani wreath over her black hair that was plaited into a french braid. She walked steadily and gracefully. At her side walked Romeo with frangipani weaved into his collar. The child and the dog were the same height. They had practiced this walk many times since the family's arrival two days before the wedding. We were unnecessarily concerned about their ability to walk this walk but the two of them crossed the bridge slowly and perfectly together and arrived at the entrance to the cafe' where Reverend Sarah and I waited for them. We were relieved and proud of them. Even people who never cried at weddings melted helplessly into mush as they watched this pair, announcing a new family, a new day.

They were followed some distance by Cecily. She wore a coral colored full skirted mid calf length dress, her blond hair and the yellow flowers she carried provided the yellow to match Aida's pink and yellow plaid.

Then came the bride. Aida was dressed in pale yellow chiffon ankle length dress with full length fitted sleeves. It shimmered in the dappled sunlight. She wore multiple long draping golden colored strands of pearl beads that had been worn by both her mother and her aunt Pari at their weddings. She covered her head with her yellow and pink plaid hijab, pulled back a few inches from her hairline and beautifully draped around her shoulders and neck. Aida wanted to walk this walk alone. She said she was not being "given away," but giving freely and fully of herself. She asked four of the townspeople who happened to be standing near her as she started her walk, to accompany her across the bridge and to her waiting groom. She did not know any of them. She wanted this wedding to be a sign of community and inclusiveness, like a Loi Karthong for all of those present, an image of beauty, wisdom and unity on our passage through life.

Our vows were spoken, wedding bands exchanged and certificates signed and we kissed for the first time in public to the cheers of everybody present.

Suddenly as we looked up to wave to all those gathered, I noticed that Jahanara and Romeo were missing. How could this happen? How did they slip away without being noticed? In a sudden panic, I whispered to Aida, "Where is Jahanara?"

She shrugged her shoulders. "I don't know." I could see the frightened look in her eyes and knew that the child had not been sent on an errand of some sort.

I called out loudly to everyone present, "Does anyone know where our child has gone?"

My panic was transmitted to the crowd. Everyone started talking and looking around. It seemed no one had noticed her leaving. Then Charlotte pointed and called from the bridge where she was standing looking over the creek, "There she is."

"Oh my god, is she in the water? is she okay?" I couldn't even look at Aida but I grabbed her hand. This couldn't happen, not today, not ever.

"She's down by the water with the dog. She's okay I think!" Charlotte called out

We ran to the bridge to look over and there was Jahanara, all muddy, squatting by the water. She had taken the wreath of flowers off of her head and was pulling out one pedal at a time, happily throwing it on the water and watching it float away.

I said to Aida, through my astonished tears, "Loi Krathong!" She and Cecily looked at each other. We all had the same idea at the same time. On a lark, giggling from relief, we climbed down the bank to the water and threw all the flowers we had been carrying, even my boutonniere, into the moving water of the creek. We watched them float out toward the Ocoee River, toward the Ocean, out into the wide world, together.

Then we heard Oscar, who had stayed up on the bridge. He bellowed loudly to all of us who were gathered, "Champagne is poured." Laughing, Cecily picked up Jahanara and gave her a tight hug, covering her own dress with the wonderful black earth that came from Jahanara's dress and hands and face. Aida lowered her hijab to her shoulders, I grabbed Aida's hand and together we climbed up the bank toward our new life.

This book is available on Amazon.com

If you enjoyed "Flowering" watch for the next book in this series, the story of JAHANARA

Flowering

i

Made in the USA
Columbia, SC
18 July 2018